THE
FINGERED
BOY
KU-008-224

THE TWELVE-FINGERED BOY

JOHN HORNOR JACOBS

carolrhoda LAB
MINNEAPOLIS

Carolrhoda Lab™
An imprint of Carolrhoda Books
A division of Lerner Publishing Group, Inc.
241 First Avenue North
Minneapolis, MN 55401 USA

For reading levels and more information, look up this title at www.lernerbooks.com.

Main body text set in Janson Text Lt Std 11/15.
Typeface provided by Linotype AG.

Library of Congress Cataloging-in-Publication Data

Jacobs, John Hornor.
The twelve-fingered boy / John Hornor Jacobs.
p. cm. — (The Twelve-Fingered Boy Trilogy.)
Summary: Fifteen-year-old fast-talking Shreve is thriving in juvenile detention until he is assigned a strangely silent and vulnerable new cellmate, Jack, who just might have superpowers and who attracts the attention both of the cellblock bullies and sinister Mr. Quincrux.
ISBN: 978-0-7613-9007-7 (trade hard cover : alk. paper)
ISBN: 978-1-4677-0950-7 (eBook)
[1. Juvenile detention homes—Fiction. 2. Supernatural—Fiction. 3. Ability—Fiction. 4. Bullies—Fiction.] I. Title.
PZ7.J152427Twe 2013
[Fic]—dc23 2012015292

Manufactured in the United States of America
2 – BP – 12/31/13

FOR ADAM RULE

THE BROTHER I CHOOSE

PART ONE:
INCARCERADO

O God, I could be bounded in a nutshell and count myself a king of infinite space, were it not that I have bad dreams.

— *Hamlet*, Act II, Scene 2, by William Shakespeare

A human being is part of a whole, called by us "Universe," a part limited in time and space. He experiences himself, his thoughts and feelings, as something separated from the rest, a kind of optical delusion of his consciousness. This delusion is a kind of prison for us, restricting us to our personal desires and to affection for a few persons nearest us. Our task must be to free ourselves from this prison by widening our circles of compassion to embrace all living creatures and the whole of nature in its beauty.

— Albert Einstein

ONE

On the inside, everyone's the same. From the worst offenders—the kids who've killed, shot their parents, mutilated their pets, terrorized their neighbors—to the druggies and potheads, the dealers and the oxymorons. From the junior gangbangers, the bandanna wranglers, to the saddest wards of the state, the titty-babies, popped for serial shoplifting and curfew violations—they're all the same.

They all love candy. They'll eat that crap until their teeth rot out.

That's where I come in.

▪▪▪

He's standing by the water fountain, picking his nose with the pad of his thumb. Not really digging into the nostril, just kind of brushing it the way adults do. They like to think it's not really picking your nose if you don't use your index finger. It is, actually. Assistant Warden Horace Booth stops, peeks at his thumb, and flicks his fingers like he had crumbs on them instead of boogs. Then he places his hands on his waist with the general I'm-king-of-the-world attitude that I've become used to. He watches the general pop, watches the boys playing dominoes, the boys reading, the boys yukking it up. He watches, always vigilant, always there to make sure we don't go all *Lord of the Flies* and start sacrificing kids.

I've got the conch. He knows it, I know it.

Ox, who's partial to Blow Pops, keeps his bulk between Booth and me so I can make the deal. Some kids got the jones for hard candy. Some kids got the jones for chocolate. Some are devils for gum and the chewy stuff. Now and Laters. Jujyfruits. Gummi Bears. Some are just big, walking cavities waiting to happen. And to get it, they'll pay. If I'm shadowing Ox, none of the D-Wing goons will bother me, even if I'm holding, and none of the C-Wing cadre will dare try to rough me up. Ox's ugly face, sprouting a Blow Pop stem, is enough to scare off even the toughest delinquent. And he's just sixteen, tall and muscled like his namesake. Don't know his real name.

Kenny, seeing the deal's about to go down, sidles up and slips me the cash. I don't even need to count it to know it's there. It's there, or he'll never get another pack of Sweet Tarts for the next two years, which is how long I'll be in here. Kenny's due a longer haul for robbing that little old granny at the five-and-dime. When he laughs about his arrest—his bust, he calls it—the way the old lady cried as the police arrived, you can see his black, nasty teeth. The boy don't brush.

And why should he? No mothers in Casimir Pulaski Juvenile Detention Center for Boys to tell you to brush your teeth. No fathers to tell you to floss—not like that was a problem for me before, on the outside. Just Assistant Warden Booth, watching and waiting.

Brushing your teeth isn't in the rule book. Dealing candy is. If he catches me, I'm bound for the Farm. At the Farm I have no contacts—no cousin who'll slip me the goods, who'll stash a box of candy in caches around old Casimir Juvie.

(You think I'm gonna tell you where? Right. Think again—if it don't hurt you too much.)

At the Farm there's just fields and dirt and backbreaking labor moving rocks or crap like that, surrounded by hardened, violent juvenile offenders. I've seen the brochure. It ain't pretty.

I'm a city mouse. I just wouldn't fit in.

Kenny kneels to tie his shoe and waits. Hand in my pocket, I release the pack of oversized chewy Sweet Tarts. It slides down my leg, slows at the cuff, and peeks out on top of my Chuck T. I flip it with my foot. Kenny nabs it out of the air, easy-peasy, and strolls off.

I whistle.

Ox nods, saunters over to a domino game with some of the fellas from B Wing, laughing, slapping knees.

It takes Booth maybe two seconds to see me. His eyes get narrow.

I could ignore him, but why? This is the game we play. I walk over.

"Afternoon, Assistant Warden Booth. How's tricks?"

Booth glowers. "I've been looking for you, Shreve. You

can get away with it for days, even weeks, but eventually, you'll make a mistake. And then . . ."

He chuckles. Not my favorite sound in the world.

"The Farm," I say, just to steal some of his thunder. "Yeah, we've been over this before."

Booth points to the sign over the locked double doors that lead to Admin.

"You know what that says, boy?"

"*Parens patriae*."

"You know what it means?"

"Someone thought they were clever to put up a sign no one can read."

I don't know, but he might purple a little bit at that one.

Booth withdraws a comb, one of the ones with a tight little black fist, from his back pocket and picks at his hair. Whatever is wrong with Booth, it's true he's got nice hair. Neat little pencil-thin mustache. He's a well-groomed man. Rings. Puffed out chest like a peacock. Still, he picks his nose in public. The fact he doesn't think it's picking his nose doesn't matter.

When he's done with his comb, he tucks it back in his pocket, looks at me, and says, "It means, while you're in here . . ." He jabs a pink-nailed, manicured finger at the old flagstones of the Pulaski County Juvenile Detention Center floor. "While you're in here, I'm your daddy."

He's read my profile, so he's got me at a disadvantage. But I'll be damned if I let him see how much that smarts.

"Well, it's been nice talking to you, Assistant Warden, but I've got an appointment with the state shrink about the abuse that goes on in here . . ."

Booth puts his hand on my shoulder, gently, as I walk away.

"No, Shreve. You don't. Come with me."

"Where we going? You can't search me without another warden and a state psychologist present. State law."

He shakes his head, exasperated.

"Cripes, boy. I thought you were smarter than that. I know you wouldn't just walk over here, bold as brass, if you had contraband on you." He gives me a look like he's a little disappointed in me. Weird, but it hurts some that I didn't live up to his expectations. There's a contract between enemies. To do your best.

"I've got a surprise for you."

"What?"

"You'll see. Come on."

He walks off toward B Wing, land of my assigned room. When you're incarcerado at Casimir Juvie, you're not put in a cell. Just a bare-ass room with shatterproof windows and an automatic lock on the magic door that opens and shuts by itself. Metal bunk beds. Two metal dressers. A desk fastened tight to the wall. Two backless chairs—stools, really. A doorless bathroom with a stainless-steel mirror like you see in the toilets at public parks: unbreakable, but dimpled with dents from the idiots who have to try. No ceramics in our bathroom. Nothing breakable at all. Nothing you could cut your wrists with, cut your roommate's throat with. Not quite prison. Not quite a Hilton.

Booth jangles as he walks, his key ring making bright sounds that ping off the tile walls, the windows, the green tile floors reeking of Pine-Sol, the fluorescent lights ticking and flickering above us.

He opens doors, I step through the metal detectors with no beeps, and we enter B Wing. B Wing is two floors with an atrium. It's pretty much what you'd expect of a penitentiary, but with doors instead of bars. They doors are open today, and sun streams down from the skylights. It's a nice day outside.

They try to spruce it up a little bit so we don't get all emo or psychotic in here, without family. Or fathers. They paint the walls different colors. Sometimes they let an artist come in to paint a mural, usually so hideous we have a ball making fun of it.

Up the stairs Booth leads, jangling. He stops at my door, 14, and I hear the soft sounds of Warden Kay Anderson chatting inside my room.

Booth opens the door, and there she is, sitting on the lower bunk next to a small, dark-haired boy. He's twelve, thirteen maybe, and looking around at the bare walls, bewildered, lost.

I nudge Booth with my elbow and say out of the side of my mouth, "Hey, shouldn't this fish be in a foster home? He's not quite Casimir material."

Booth grunts, jangles. "He was in a foster home. Put five kids in the hospital."

"Right," I say. "When you're done yanking my chain, tell me why you're sticking me with the titty-baby."

Booth ignores me and gives a little shove between my shoulder blades, pushing me into the room.

Warden Anderson looks up and smiles in that brittle way she has, like she wants to be nice and motherly, but she really doesn't have the time or inclination for it. So, instead, she's going to do her best to smile. And damned if she doesn't. She smiles wide, showing yellowed teeth smeared with lipstick, to show me I'm absolutely, positively, the most important ward of the state.

"Oh, Shreve, I'm glad you're here," she says. "I want you to meet your new cellmate—"

Booth coughs. The Warden glances at Booth.

"I'm sorry. I meant to say roommate. Here. Him. Shreve Cannon, meet Jack Graves. I hope you two will enjoy your time together." She stands, smooths her skirt. Then she runs her hand over her gigantic, bulky belt. It's not quite business casual, like the rest of her. First she touches the pepper spray. Then she moves to the coils of zip ties and touches the walkie-talkie. She lingers on each one in turn, stopping for a while on the handcuffs as if she's considering hitching me to the titty-baby. Then, finally, she comes to rest on the Taser at her hip. She's looking at me with the harried yet official stare of an administrator. The Administrator, the boss-lady. It's not that I don't exist to her. I exist. But I'm only one little gear in the great machine that is Casimir Pulaski Juvenile Detention Center for Boys. And by God, she's here to make sure that machine has oil applied to all the squeaky parts.

Booth blinks at the warden, glances at me, and shrugs. She looks around the room with an expression that says she's disappointed in me, maybe, or in her situation. But for the moment it'll have to do. We all make compromises, so let's just get to business.

"All right, then," the Warden says. "You'll handle the rest?"

"Yes, ma'am."

"Good. Let me know how it goes."

She walks to the door, stops, and turns to me.

"Shreve, I almost forgot." She turns, puts her heels together like she'd been in the Army or something. "Empty out your pockets. Now. And let me warn you, if you refuse, you'll spend the next eight hours in an examination room, waiting for the state psychologist to arrive. Without food, or water, or sleep. So that we can discover what you have secreted about your person." She pauses and then runs her eyes up and down my frame. She shifts her grip on her Taser. "We'll search everywhere. Most likely your orifices, too. You never know. Booth tells me you sell a large amount of candy to the other wards . . . Lord knows how you get the candy. But we mean to find out. Don't we, Horace?" Booth grunts again. "We must be wary that you haven't moved on to harder stuff."

Sometimes my mouth works without me controlling it.

"Like what? Pop Rocks?"

"Well . . ." She's heard all this before from a million kids with smart mouths and bad haircuts. She's not annoyed or angry. She's seen it all before. "Drugs," she says, simply enough. "Weed. Meth. Oxy. X. We must be sure you don't have any hidden in your . . ." She blinks and looks a bit embarrassed that the situation has come to this. "Your bottom."

She smiles. It's an apologetic one, the smile. It's an Oh-I'm-So-Sorry-We-Have-To-Search-What-You-Have-In-Your-Bottom kind of smile.

I turn out my pockets.

There's lint and the money Kenny gave me for the Sweet Tarts. Nothing else.

The Warden looks it over, blinks, and then turns and marches out of the cell, her heels clicking. She leaves behind a faint scent of dead flowers and vinegar.

Booth shakes his head.

"I thought you were gonna make an ass of yourself there, boy."

I look at the new kid. He's slight, pale, and still. More still than most people. You see folks, adults, kids—whether they're wearing a uniform or an orange jumpsuit, they're busy, never still. People jitter. They tap their feet or twiddle their thumbs. Or pick their noses, even though they don't think it's nose-picking.

But not this kid. This Jack. He just stands, hands at his sides, his big brown eyes taking it all in. His eyes are the only things that move, going between Booth, me, the door, his bunk. He's not wary, but yet not calm either. He's waiting.

I can't take much more of it, so I stick out my hand to shake.

"Name's Shreve. I got the top bunk."

He stuffs his hands into his pockets.

"I'm Jack. Nice to meet you."

Booth laughs, pats me on the shoulder. "Have fun, boys," he says. I hear him jangle himself away in the Warden's wake.

Jack turns in a still, almost formal way, like he was a butler or something, and lies down on the bottom bunk.

Weird kid.

TWO

On the inside, everyone's got a story.

Take Ox, for instance. His daddy gave him boxing gloves for Christmas. So Ox set up a fight club in his backyard. Beat ten, maybe fifteen, kids senseless. That wouldn't have been a problem if he hadn't taken their money and sneakers as forfeit while he was at it. He figured he deserved something for whipping them.

One kid, that one kid, Ox broke his face pretty good. Blood stopped flowing in places it needed to flow, and the brain went a little wonky. Now the kid gets soup fed to him three times a day through a straw and craps in a bag. The rest of the time he drools and moans. Not exactly what he expected when he pulled on the boxing gloves.

I doubt he knew Ox's name was Ox.

▪▪▪

I wonder what Jack's story is. He doesn't talk much. He just holds his body still and remains polite, lying on his bunk.

"Yo. Jack. Where you from?"

Booth calls for headcount, so I don't wait for Jack's answer. I hop down off the top bunk, motion to Jack to get up, and we move outside the door. I stand beside the door and point to Jack's spot on the other side. Boys, both across the empty space of the atrium and along our wall, step out and take position like sentries.

Booth strolls down the walkway.

"Where's Miller?" he hollers to the general pop.

"Infirmary." That's Berman. He's a good customer. A fiend for the gooey stuff, with a taste for Gummi Bears.

"Right. I'll have to speak with the day guard."

Booth jangles down the line, marking our presence on a clipboard as he goes. Once he makes the line and all are accounted for, he jangles back toward us and heads down the stairs. At the bottom he bellows, "Fifteen till lights out! Fifteen! Brush your damned teeth, boys, before Shreve rots them out!"

There's a smattering of laughter. I smile, showing it doesn't bother me. But he'll get his, that Booth.

We go back in the room, and Jack lies down again and rolls over, facing the wall, hugging himself.

I hop back up to my bunk. I adjust the air conditioning vent so it points right at me. I like it cold.

"So, Jack." The vent squeaks a little with the adjustment. "Where you from?"

"Little Rock."

"That's where I'm from, too. Where'd you go?"

Silence. Maybe he's slow. Didn't understand the question.

"School, you know? I went to Pulaski Heights. The Panthers. Rah rah. You?"

"Home."

"Home? Whatdya mean?"

"Home schooling. I never went to school."

"You mean you just stayed at home? Didn't go to school?"

After that he stops talking, even when I prod. When I peek over the edge at the bottom bunk, he's facing the wall, curled up. Maybe he's asleep.

Whatever.

I read comics until I hear Booth's voice calling lights-out and the door, my cell door, swings shut as though pushed by an invisible hand. There's the click that indicates we're locked down for the night.

I feel more than hear the new kid shift, look around the darkened room, and then settle.

I remember my first night. Hard to forget something like that.

"Hey, Jack."

Silence.

"It isn't that bad. Okay? Might look bad now. But it's not."

Hell, I don't know how to soothe a titty-baby.

More silence. Which skeeves me a little. Why can't the kid react like a normal person, especially when someone's trying to help him out?

He might have fallen asleep. Could be. Maybe not.

Hell, I don't know.

I wait, breathing slow. The trick is to make him think from my breathing that I'm asleep, but to stay awake and not let the deep breathing lull me down into the mattress. Into the pillow.

When I'm sure Jack's asleep, I sit up, tilt my head toward the air vent where the wall meets the ceiling, and put my mouth at the grate.

"Ox. You there, hoss?"

I hear a little echo, maybe Ox adjusting the vent.

"Yeah. I told you not to call me that."

"What? Ox?"

"Naw. Hoss. It's like you're saying I'm stupid or something."

"It's just a turn of phrase, bigun. But fine. I'll stick to Ox. You know, like a farm animal. That cool? How's that for you?"

"Shreve, one of these days . . ."

"What? When you get sick of candy? When you get tired of stuffing chocolate bars down your hole? One of these days what?"

"Man, you don't have to be so uncool." He pauses. "Uncool, man."

He's thicker than a cinder block, but he's got a point. He's a hoss, a farm animal, and I shouldn't whip him so hard.

"Listen, Ox." I like the lug. I do. I like what he does for me. I try to put that into my voice. I hope it'll carry through the vent. "I'm sorry, pard. Look. I scored a load of Heath bars. I know you love that toffee stuff. I got a couple with your name on it." There's a scratching and then an exhalation of air. Hard to tell if it's the AC kicking on or if Ox is just mouth-breathing again.

"I like toffee."

"That's good, bro. Real good. I'll hit you up tomorrow. But I need you to run interference at midday Commons. And work escort right before lights out. Can you handle that? Two Heaths and a couple of Blow Pops?"

There's a gurgle at the other end of the vent. The blockhead is probably drooling on his chest like some Russian dog.

Before Ox can answer there's a chuff, and the air kicks on. I lie back on the bed and wait, hands cradled behind my head, working out the deals for tomorrow.

▪▪▪

On the inside, some folks don't know what they want. Some folks have to be convinced they want what you got. Some folks have to be convinced they don't want what you got. You have to scare them bad enough that they don't think they can take it from you. It's only been six months since I first came here, but now I can't remember if the inside differs from the way it is outside. I doubt it really matters. I'm on the inside, and I'll remain incarcerado for the next eighteen months.

And the new kid? That Jack? How's he going to figure into my plans?

I'm fading to black, the air blowing above me, through the vent, out into the room, like darkness.

▪▪▪

It's morning. There's a buzz, and the door clicks and swings open. I hear boys whooping, cawing like crows, rapping homespun lyrics, mumbling, cursing as they roll out of their cells, getting ready for headcount. You can be a blind man in Casimir Juvie and still be able to function fine on scent and sound.

I figured Booth would be here to give Jack the lowdown as to Casimir operations, but no dice. I've got to hold the little bugger's hand.

I hop down and grab the least stinky jumpsuit from the dresser. Bright orange, baby. Nothing rhymes with it. Nothing matches it.

The kid doesn't look like he's slept at all. I wonder.

He sits on his bed, looking like he doesn't want to stand. I'm tugging on the jumpsuit, pulling the sleeves over my arms.

"Look, they gave you the suit. So suit up. I'll show you the mess hall. The food ain't that bad." I zip. "They've got to feed us pretty well—otherwise, lawsuits. You know. Kids."

Jack looks at me, tries to smile, fails, and then moves over to his dresser and takes out . . . guess what? . . . an orange jumper. I move on to the can and scrubbing the teeth. I might sample my own product, but I make sure the pearly whites get clean. Nothing inspires confidence like a toothless candy man.

I come back in the room, and Jack's standing there, trying to zip up his jumper, hands tugging at the tab.

"They stick, the zippers, until they've been washed a couple times. You got to grab the belly fabric and rip up." I'm moving to help the kid when I see his fingers. Something's weird there. Jack struggles to zip his jumper, and I'm standing there looking at his hands.

I pull on my own jumper, over the greys of underwear and T-shirt, and then look back at Jack still struggling.

"You've really got to pull up hard . . ." I say. Looking again at his hands. He notices me looking at him, and he quickly turns his back. But not before I can get a count.

"Holy crow," I breathe. There's not much else to say. The kid's got extra fingers. They're not stumpy or anything. His hands look normal. Just extra fingers. "Your hands."

Jack stops trying to zip and puts his hands behind his back.

"Jack. Holy crap. Your hands. You got like a gajillion fingers. What's up with—"

He says nothing. Big surprise there. I move closer, wanting to see.

"Jack, it's cool. I just want to look. At the fingers, man. You could be in the circus or something. Let me see."

Then something weird happens. The air in front of Jack wavers—like heat fumes on the highway in summer, when you're riding in a car and looking far ahead—and I feel a slight draft. I can feel a pressure on my chest, my arms, my thighs, and my face. It's a wind, but it's not a wind either. It's slower and more concentrated, and I'm slowly, slowly pushed backward into the wall between the door to the bathroom and our beds. With the wall at my back, the pressure on my chest builds and builds. I can feel something like my ribs cracking, and I'm having a hard time breathing now. Jack looks scared, like he knows what's happening. Then he barks out a word, "No!" The pressure eases, and I'm on my knees, gasping for breath.

Jack rushes over and grabs me. He takes my hand and pulls me up—he's stronger than he looks, the little dude—and drags me over to his bunk. I flop on my back, gasping, feeling at my ribs to make sure nothing's gone crunchy. They feel okay.

"I'm sorry, Shreve. I'm sorry. I didn't mean to." Jack keeps repeating this, and I don't even know what's going on. I'm going to get pissed off if he starts to cry. Which might happen. It looks like the waterworks are primed.

"Nothing, man. It's nothing. Asthma attack, I guess. Used to get 'em when I was younger. You know. Moms is a smoker."

Jack's shaking his head, looking down at me. But he doesn't argue. I don't know what the hell just happened. I looked at his hands; then things got crazy.

His fingers. I can see his hands clearly now. He has twelve fingers, six to a hand. They look so normal you'd never notice unless you were looking directly at them. Weird.

Jack sees me looking, sees me counting.

He swallows. Starts to say something. Stops. Starts again.

"It's cool, Jack. You got fingers. Big deal. Ox is freakish large." Jack winces at the word *freakish*. I have a way with words, you know? Words are my thing. That's how you sell. How you survive in a world full of people like Ox, people wanting to take from you everything you have. But I probably shouldn't say stuff like that to Jack.

"I was born this way. It's not like I chose to have twelve fingers. Please don't tell. People will get hurt."

I think about this. Jack didn't ask for the extra fingers. I didn't ask for a sloppy-drunk mother or a ghost for a father. But we got them, didn't we? We got them. Ox, on the other hand, could try not to look so damned ugly and beat on folks. However, if he did that, he wouldn't be any use to me. So there's that.

But the kid is different. You can find guys as large and as tough as Ox in every block. Ringo from E Wing is as stout, and Ponty from D is as tall. But twelve fingers . . . that goes beyond the population of Casimir Pulaski Juvenile Detention Center for Boys. It goes beyond my experience.

He's a rare bird, this Jack. But what does it mean?

"Yeah." Might as well be honest with him. He seems like a cool guy if you can get past the silences. "It's a monster of a world, always giving us gifts we don't want. Don't worry, your secret is safe with me."

Jack smiles then. He's obviously not used to doing it, and the smile is an uneasy one. But it changes the whole configuration of his face, the smile.

"Thanks, Shreve." He exhales. "Thank you. You don't know how bad it can get—"

"I got an idea, pard." I cough and stand up. My stomach grumbles a bit, and I'm reminded breakfast is waiting. "I've lived with a clown for a mother since I was little. I know how it feels to be in the circus."

Jack nods. He looks at his hands and then back up to me.

"I didn't know my parents." He's not shooting for sympathy; he's not angry, not anything. It's just plain fact.

I clap him on the shoulder. "Hell, Jack, you're not missing anything there. Trust me on this one."

He tries to laugh and fails.

I guess I do, too. Not as funny as I thought it was.

Then Sloe-Eyed Norman calls for headcount, and we take position outside our door.

THREE

On the inside, where all the wards wear orange, everyone tries to be different. Some with crazy dos, some wearing earrings, the more desperate scratching tats on their hands with black pen ink and needles. Kids talk big, walk big, kick out their chests, tell jokes in overloud voices, laugh hard at unfunny jokes. They try to put a stamp down on themselves. They want to define who they are, and who they aren't, by drawing lines in an ever-changing sandbox.

But the ones who are different, the ones who really would stand out if their differences were known to the general pop, well . . . they don't want to be different at all. They want to be just like everybody else. The boys so desperately trying to be different, well, if they get a whiff of something truly foreign, they'll destroy it. Nothing that different can be allowed to exist, to prove that they're all alike.

■ ■ ■

Jack is scared. It doesn't take a mind reader to know he's worried about the integrity of his skin.

We walk down B Wing's center, through the bull gates. Sloe-Eyed Norman checks off the headcount. The sweetheart, he grins and waves us through, raising a sleepy eyebrow at Jack. Once we're in the Commons, the ruckus starts. Big Paulie from A Wing is arguing with Ernie from D about dominoes. They've got M&M's on the table, so it's a serious conversation.

"That ain't the play, Ernie! Ain't your play. It's my play."

"Stow that, you damned tool. It ain't your play just because you say it's your play. Prove it."

Paulie states his first argument, a brilliant little piece of logic. He punches Ernie right in the maw, pushing Ernie back onto another table and sending plastic chairs scattering and tumbling, like, well . . . dominoes.

But Ernie pops right back up, wiping the blood streaming from his lip and nose with the back of his hand, like a prizefighter. His eyes bright, he begins his retort. There's a jab, a jab, a hook, pretty much by the book, with Paulie making little weaving motions with his head, trying to reach in there. Ernie's hunched up, getting low, and delivering blows to Paulie's gut.

I back up. It's about to get ugly.

Paulie hits Ernie hard, right on the cheekbone. Ernie's eyes roll back in his head—not as a prelude to unconsciousness, but as a harbinger of pure berserker rage. The nicey-nice fistfight is over. Ernie's eyes snap forward. He throws himself on top of Paulie, biting, grabbing hair, gouging eyes, bearing the larger boy to the ground. Paulie howls, inventing curses, throwing elbows, kicking out with his feet, swinging his head around like a rhino looking for something to butt.

I peek at Jack. He remains motionless. He's got his hands in his pockets, so it gives him this casual appearance that contradicts the expression on his face. He's hiding his hands. How often do you look, really *look*, at someone's hands? I see them because I *know*, but despite the extra fingers, they're perfectly formed and it takes a moment to even come to grips with the number. You have to be paying attention, looking at them. He can cough, or grab something, and you'd never even notice . . . but once you do, you'll never *not* notice.

"These knuckleheads will be at it for a while. Don't worry, the bulls will break them up before any permanent damage. And maybe, who knows? Maybe one of them will end up at the Farm. C'mon, I'm hungry."

Jack blinks and falls in beside me, hands still in pockets.

In the mess hall we get our trays, fill our plates with powdered eggs, grits, bacon, and biscuits with little packages of grape jelly. There are tiny tubs of strawberry jam with peel-off tops, too. I've never been able to figure out what's the difference between jelly and jam. It puzzles me.

Ox sits next to some of his C-Wing compadres. I wander over, motion to Jack to sit down, and I put myself between him and Ox.

Reasoner pops in, slings his tray halfway across the table, and sits down. "It's like *Clash of the Titans* out there, boys. Ernie and Big P have gotten into a tussle. Ernie's eating Paulie's lunch." Reasoner speaks mostly in reference to movies.

Another kid, I don't know his name, pipes up: "Had a couple of bags of M&M's out there on the table. The pot looked pretty rich."

"There'll be big trouble in little China if the bulls get wind of the candy whereabouts." Reasoner looks at me. Why doesn't he just announce it?

His prices just went up.

"What? They can talk all they want, but I'm just a bystander, Greasy. I have nothing to do with that fight."

Reasoner snorts. It makes me want to choke the sound out of him. But he's wiry and mean, and I might get the bad end of that deal.

Ox eats. He uses both hands—one clutching a biscuit, the other sprouting a fork. He's got big, ungainly fists. Even with six fingers per, Jack's got more articulate mitts. Ox makes short work of the grub. Swipe: two tons of eggs down the hatch. Swipe: a shovelful of grits. He peers over my head at Jack.

"Who's the fish, Shreve?"

"New roommate. Everybody, meet Jack. Jack, meet everybody."

The boys murmur hellos over one another, and Ox says, "Niceta. He gonna mess up our deal?"

"No, he's cool, Ox. He's cool."

Jack's doing his possum routine. Whenever anyone

speaks to him, he hides his hands in his lap and goes still. Like a rock. Which isn't going to cut it. The more he does that, the more the boys will pay attention.

I whisper, "Hey. You gotta talk, or they'll get curious. And you don't want that."

Jack looks at me, mouth open, eyes wide. He's like the poster child for the Big Surprise Foundation. I bark a little laugh around a spoonful of grits, and flecks of white fly from my mouth, out over the table.

"Hey!" Reasoner yanks his tray back. "What is this, *Animal House* or something?"

Kent, from down the table, says, "Hey, Greasoner, you seen any movies from this century?"

"Yeah. And they all suck."

Jack clears his throat. "Hey. Um. You guys seen *Demon Down*?"

Reasoner guffaws. "Sure, guy, sure. They had a special screening with the director and all the stars right in Commons."

Jack flushes so deep I can feel the heat from his skin like a radiator.

Ox mumbles, "You seen it, Jack?"

"Yeah. It's good."

"That chick in it? The one with the bumps." Ox holds his hands in front of his chest like he's cradling a watermelon.

"Yes." Jack shifts in his seat. "Temple Wrath. She's amazing."

Other boys start craning their heads to get a load of Jack. He puts his hands on the table. He's curling the extra fingers into his palm.

"What about the demon things? They ugly?"

"Yeah. But there's very little CGI in this movie. So . . ." Jack gestures at Reasoner. "It's more like an older movie. Like one from the eighties. Or before."

"Sounds like *The Thing*. Buckets of goo and prosthetics."

Jack nods. He's doing his best to act excited. "It's awesome. They take on any form they touch. They eat people from the feet up. The head down. It's crazy."

"Heard there's some ugly bumping, you know, between Temple and Brad."

Jack nods. "Shower scene. It's . . . it's really steamy. You can't see much, but what you can see . . ."

I don't know Jack. No truer words have ever been spoken. But I know Jack better than these lunkheads, and I can hear the deadness in his voice. He might have seen the movie, he might have appreciated it in some fashion, but he didn't like it. I don't know if our boy Jack is even able to like anything. His voice is dead.

But he does a passable imitation of a real boy.

I have to wonder, what's his story? He's been hurt, hurt bad, over and over again, seems like. You just don't have that hard a time smiling, or that hard a time describing some movie star's knockers, unless you've been hurt bad. It doesn't take a mind reader to see it.

I have a brother. Name's Vigor. The little dude doesn't

come to see me—too young. He's stuck with Moms. Dealing with her, I guess. And by the time I get out of here, he won't be a little dude anymore. He'll be a piece of old charcoal. He'll be hard-eyed from mopping up Moms's puke, putting out her cigarettes before they burn down the trailer park. He'll be crusty from cooking and cleaning. From doing all the things a mom blotto from Ancient Age or nipply vodka isn't able to do for herself. And he won't be my little dude anymore. He'll sound like Jack.

I pat Jack on the shoulder. It's not much, but it's all I can do to let him know he's done good. He looks at his food, then looks at the boys surrounding us, each one nose-down in his cafeteria tray. Jack snatches up his fork and scoops up some eggs, pops them in his mouth, drops the fork and brings his hands into his lap. Like a bird darting in for breadcrumbs, fast and inconspicuous. He waits, watching, and then grabs a biscuit and takes a huge bite, drops it and places his hands in his lap. It's kinda amazing, really, how practiced his movements are. Everything is done quickly, like a turtle's head snaking out to nab a passing fish, then back into the shell.

There comes a jangling and footsteps.

"You boys smell that?" I say, loud enough for the room to hear. "Smells like they're cooking another batch of bacon. Mmmm. Pig." I rub my stomach.

I look behind me, dramatically.

"Oh, I'm sorry, Assistant Warden. I didn't realize it was you."

Reasoner, Ox, and the rest snicker. Booth's little pencil-thin mustache quivers with anger.

"Jack, I need you to come with me."

Behind Booth is a nondescript man in a black suit. I say he's nondescript because I can see that's what he wants me to think. I don't know how I know this, but I do. He's not tall, not short, not thin, not fat. Sandy brown hair. Clear complexion. Totally unremarkable. But I'm remarking on him. I see him; I see through what he wants everyone to see.

He's holding a briefcase and looking at Jack, looking at him hard. I glance from the man back to Jack. Jack's twisted in his seat to stare at the new arrivals. But his hands are hidden.

I look back to the suited man—he's got a keen stare, and he's not paying attention to anything or anyone except Jack.

"Why?" I ask.

"Not your business, Cannon." Booth snaps his fingers, as if that means anything. Another one of his little, impotent gestures. "Jack, Mr. Quincrux needs to speak with you."

Quincrux. The name comes to my mouth, and I whisper it to get the taste. A strange name. But when I look at the suited man, I know—don't ask me how—I know this is his true name. It's like I'm tuned into a certain frequency, the same frequency he's broadcasting, and I just know like a radio knows crappy country music or windbag sports announcers.

Jack stands, puts his hands in his pockets.

I have a bad feeling about this. This Quincrux, he has the same stillness as Jack. He holds his body motionless, hands dangling along with the briefcase at his sides. The only movement of his body is the rise and fall of his chest and his eyes scouring Jack.

"You don't have to go, pard. You can refuse, demand a lawyer or psychologist. They can't make you."

Quincrux's gaze shifts, clicking over to me like machinery, cold but now mildly interested. Mildly.

I look back. I try to give him the grin that I've worked on for so long, the one that says, *I know something you don't.* The one that makes Booth livid. The one that makes Moms outraged when she's desperate and drunk. I try to give the smile to Quincrux, but it curdles under his gaze and I feel a kaleidoscope of emotions and images rising in me. I want to laugh, to cry, to rage and hit someone. I close my eyes, and my mother swims up from the deep. I see my old girlfriend Coco, my brother Vigor. Then our trailer, my old school, our dog, Cookie—the puppy that was pancaked on the interstate. Like cards being shuffled, they come to my mind's eye. For a moment, I worry that the food I've eaten has gone rancid and is causing hallucinations.

When my eyes open, Quincrux stands motionless, looking at me. The images continue to come, like ghosts overlaid on top of the visible world. Ox. Booth. Anderson. A phantom image of Jack hovers over Quincrux, superimposed and insubstantial.

I close my eyes again, and this time I push back with all my might. I try to think of something hard and unbreakable.

A bright blue jawbreaker.

I imagine teeth trying to crunch it, to tap its sweetness. But it's diamond-hard, and the teeth scrape and then crumble away.

I open my eyes and see Quincrux's eyes widen, just a little. Not enough for anyone else to notice, but I see. I see him. And he saw me. More than I've ever let anyone see.

Booth says, "Mr. Quincrux is from the Department of Health and Human Services. Sorry, Shreve, but he's allowed to interview all wards of the state. It's law." Booth gives me a smile, and the kicker is he's not being smart or smarmy or snide with it. He's just smiling at me because, I don't know, he's happy.

Jack looks at me, eyes wide, and nods in a way that's part acceptance, part thanks. He smiles, too, and this time his smiling doesn't seem to take an effort.

"It's okay, Shreve. I'll be all right."

I'll be damned. The kid is reassuring me.

He pulls his leg from the cafeteria bench and walks, straight-backed, to where Quincrux and Booth wait. They turn and head back to Commons, Jack in tow.

FOUR

On the inside, getting what you want requires giving up something you value. I guess that's the same as the outside, but I can't remember exactly. "Ox, I need to get into your room. You've got to get me in."

"Why?"

"Because if they're gonna question Jack, I've got to hear."

"Nah. It's almost time for English. Mr. Allenby will be pissed if we're not there. Demerits. And I don't want to work the kitchen again this month."

On the inside, like the outside, you can do what you can get away with, but eventually someone will make you pay.

"Listen. It's weird, son. That Mr. Quincrux is . . . he's different. He made me . . . I don't know . . . feel weird."

"He turn you on or something?"

For a split second, I imagine punching Ox right in his fat mouth. But the anger goes away quick enough, replaced by the urge to continue breathing—which I wouldn't be doing if I punched him in the face.

And my teachers say I've got poor impulse control.

"No. Listen. Listen. He looked at me and read my mind. He just picked my history right out of my head. Until I stopped him."

"That right?" Ox picks up his tray, waves at Reasoner and the boys, and heads toward the slop bin. Not much slop left on his tray.

"Dammit, Ox. Listen to me. If they question Jack in our cell, I need to be able to listen."

"Nah. Mr. Allenby'll give me demerits."

"He's got twelve fingers, man." It just pops right out there, without me even thinking. It's like my mouth is disconnected from my brain. It doesn't even make any sense. What does that have to do with anything?

So much for impulse control.

"The dude in the suit?"

I pause. I've said it, and there's no way to take it back.

"No. Jack. And that's why I think Quincrux is here to question him. I need your cell. So I can listen."

"You telling me the fish has twelve fingers?"

"Yeah, man. Twelve fingers."

"Wow."

Ox turns and begins shambling, not toward Commons but toward the classrooms.

"Ox! I'm not messing around here. I need in your cell."

"Nah. Mr. Allenby will be pissed."

"Two Blow Pops."

"Nah."

"Two Blow Pops. Two Heath bars."

"Two more Heath bars. On top of escort pay."

"Right. Agreed."

"Okay. Let's go."

I don't know if I'm more pissed at Ox for outmaneuvering me or at myself for spilling the beans on Jack.

"Ox, don't tell anybody else about Jack. Please. He's just a kid."

"What? Oh. Yeah. That's fine."

"Really?"

"Really what?"

"You won't tell anyone?"

"Anyone what?"

"Exactly."

"What?"

▪▪▪

Sloe-Eyed Norman waves us back through after the metal detector grants us passage. Silence means assent. I bound up the stairs, three at a time. Ox takes them one by one, so I'm waiting for a minute before he gets to the second floor. Norman, who's neatly enclosed in a windowed booth, watches us. I wave.

Norman waves back, picks up a magazine, and starts to read. But he doesn't turn back to the Commons.

We reach Ox's room. A couple kids, Miller and Smetana, are futzing around at the end of the walkway, most likely playing craps. I can't understand why Norman lets them toss dice against the wall all morning and watches us so closely.

All the cell doors are open except for one. Mine. Jack's.

They're here, not in some Admin office or classroom. They're here.

I peek through the wire-crosshatched window. There's Jack, sitting on the bed. Quincrux sits across from him, at the desk. Booth stands facing the door.

I duck my head back, hoping Booth didn't see me.

But something's wrong. When I peeked into the room, Booth didn't react. In fact, he looked . . . I don't know. Vacant. Somewhere else.

I peek again.

"You gonna use my room, Shreve? What's up?"

I hold up a finger for silence.

Booth stands in the room, off to the side, looking at the window in a thousand-yard stare. His mouth is open, and drool is spilling from his bottom lip.

What the hell is going on here?

I turn, dash into Ox's room, and jump to the top bunk, putting my ear to the vent.

FIVE

On the inside, in the quiet of the morning, sound can travel. All it takes is a listener to give it meaning.

"An unfortunate occurrence, yes? But luckily for you, your former foster brother will live. It's possible he will walk again, too, after years of painful therapy. Does this make you happy?"

"No. Yes." Jack is quiet for a bit. I'm trying to picture the way he looks, to imagine myself in the room, sitting next to Quincrux and looking at Jack on the bed. He's tamped down his hair, and his hands are between his knees. Not exactly hidden, but out of sight.

Silence and rustling echo down the dull metal walls of the vent.

"You are not a vocal youth, this I will say."

More silence.

"I'd like to ask you to do something for me. Observe this glass of water. You see?"

"Sure. It's right there."

"Please move it, if you will."

There's a pause, and then Quincrux says, "No, no. From over there."

"How can I move it without getting close to it? That doesn't make any sense."

"No matter. Here I have a series of cards with symbols on them. I am going to hold them up, and I want you to tell me what the symbols are. Do you understand?"

"I think so."

I hear the clasps of the briefcase and then the ruffling of poster board.

"First card."

"You're not going to show it to me?"

"No. You need to divine the answer."

"Divine?"

"Perceive, then."

"How can I know what's on the card if I can't see it?"

"That is a good question. A very good question. How indeed?"

"I can't."

"Try."

"Um . . . is it a . . . square?"

"No."

"A triangle?"

"No."

"A circle?"

"No." The cards ruffle again, and Quincrux sighs. "Well, this isn't working. Is it, Mr. Graves?"

"No, it isn't. I don't understand what you want."

"Obviously not. Let us move on to other matters. The word you're searching for is polydactyl. Indeed, it is a word you've been searching for all your life. It is my honor to present it to you."

"Polydactyl? I don't understand."

"Supernumerary digits. It's a congenital condition that occurs once in every five hundred births. However, multiple instances of polydactylism in one person, well . . . this is considerably rarer. Exceedingly rare, occurring in less than one in one hundred thousand births."

"You're not really with the Department of Health and . . . whatever . . . are you?" For a moment my heart goes out to the little dude. He's showing backbone, he is. Get him, Jack.

"Ah!" Quincrux talks in the same inflectionless way Jack does. His "ah" sounds like a sigh. Like he doesn't care one whit about what's going on, he's just doing his job. Or maybe he wants to die and all life is just misery. Misery and unhappiness.

That's frightening to think about.

"No, Mr. Graves. No, I am not affiliated with the Department of Health and Human Services. Should anyone wish to contact the DHHS to confirm my employment, I say to him, feel free to exercise your curiosity. My employment will be confirmed. However, you have guessed correctly. I have never once entered the DHHS building."

There's a shifting, a cough. A grunt.

"My apologies. One moment. Allow me to readjust Mr. Booth."

"You didn't do anything."

It's Quincrux's turn to remain silent.

"Why's he just standing there like that?"

"In your case, perfect postaxial polydactylism. Perfectly symmetrical. Now, may I ask you a few personal questions? Yes?"

"I . . . I guess."

"How many toes do you have?"

"Twelve."

Holy crow. Jack's got stuff sprouting everywhere.

"Are they postaxial? Do you have two pinkies or two big toes?"

"Pinkies."

"Postaxial, then. Any malformations? Will you remove your shoes so I might see?"

After a moment, I hear the clop of a shoe dropping. In my mind's eye I can see Jack's bare feet bristling with angry toes.

"Ah! That looks uncomfortable." Quincrux chuckles, a dry sound. "Diphallia?"

"What?"

"Do you have more than one penis?"

The way Quincrux asks this, with a little trill at the end, surprises me. The suit's been deadpan this whole time, but with that question he showed his interest. He's not bored anymore.

Creep.

"I'm afraid silence is not a suitable answer. Please

disrobe so that I might observe."

"No."

"I can compel you."

"No."

Don't do it, Jack. I'm going to get Norman.

Something is happening now. I can feel it through the cinder-block walls. A struggle is going on in there, even if I can't hear anything. I'm about to jump down and get Norman when Quincrux says, "So, you are not as docile as you seem."

"I don't know what you're talking about."

"Show me your hands."

"No."

"I've seen them already, in the cafeteria. Let me examine them."

"No."

Something is building in there. Something like an electrical charge, the feeling you get standing near a transformer during a thunderstorm. It's like the walls are vibrating without moving, streaming with unseen energy.

It builds. It surges, crests, and recedes. It's like a tidal pool, sinking back into the ocean. I hear a sigh, maybe of relief, but I can't tell which of them it comes from. The man or boy.

"Hmm. Your special condition seems to . . . to . . . prevent me from using my normal methods of investigation." There's a rattle, and the clasps of the briefcase snap.

"It's regretful you are such a recalcitrant young man. I would like to leave you something. I want you to read it. Think about what it might mean, not in and of itself, but as a gift. Gifts always reveal something about the giver, do they not? I hope this gift will reveal something about the giver and the recipient."

More silence. I'm worried the AC is going to kick on and make a tornado of the vent.

"I'll let you think about it, Mr. Graves. When I return, maybe you will be more . . . how shall we say this? . . . more commodious. Yes. Commodious." I can hear Quincrux rustle, hear the clack of his wing tips as he stands and walks to the door.

"As I was saying, Mr. Booth, thank you for your time and hospitality. Mr. Graves seems to be in good psychological and physical condition."

There's another cough. Then Booth mumbles, "Huh? Wha?"

"Ah. I realize this interview must have been exceedingly tiresome for you, Mr. Booth. It's completely understandable if you drifted off."

"Yeah. Well. I."

"No matter. Young Mr. Graves and I have completed our interview. I shall return to the office and finalize this report." Quincrux makes a weird little clucking in his throat. Then he says, "However, I intend to return in a week or so with a . . . colleague. A colleague with a special skill set."

"Uh. Yeah. Okay. I'll give you the form back in my office, on your way out. You'll need to have him cleared before he can have access to Jack."

"Of course. All the *t*'s will be crossed, and the *i*'s will be dotted."

"Right."

There's a jangling, and the door clicks and swings open. Quincrux's wing tips clack and diminish as they move down the walkway, toward the stairs and Norman.

I drop from the top bunk. Ox draws on a legal pad at his desk. I can't imagine what things Ox might draw. Unicorns? Wizards? Flowers?

"I'm done, bigun."

"Okay. When will I get paid?"

"This afternoon. After the yard."

He nods once. "Don't forget."

"How could I?"

"Yeah. You don't miss a trick, there, do ya, Shreve?"

Oh. I might have missed one or two in my time.

We wait a moment to let Booth, Quincrux, and Jack pass through the metal detector, and then we follow. I have to find Jack.

I hope Ox keeps his cakehole shut.

SIX

On the inside, everybody's got a story. Even me.

▪▪▪

It was before midnight on a Saturday, and Moms was already passed out. It had been a hard one leading up to her fall. I hid the vodka. She had a stash somewhere I didn't know about.

She smoked like a chimney, keeping one square dangling from her mouth as she fiddled the next from the pack. White packs without any label on them. Like government cheese and probably tasting just as awful.

"Shree, I want to watch *Price*." Moms never called anything by its whole name. Too much effort.

She didn't slur when drunk. On the contrary, she overpronounced her words. Slowly. Carefully.

"*Price* ain't on right now, Moms. It's on in the afternoon. There's *Dancing*. You want that?"

She gave an explosive blast of air in disappointment.

I played defense all night between the booze and her trying to burn down the trailer with smokes and keeping Vig fed and happy in front of the bedroom TV. I don't know what I'd do if I didn't have TV to placate him. Or her.

His name is Ferrous Vigor Cannon. That's iron strong cannon to you and me. Hard for me to say, Ferrous. I don't know what she was smoking when she signed the birth certificate. I'm Shreveport Justice Cannon.

▪▪▪

At ten or so, Moms passed out. I took the last cigarette from her fingers and stubbed it in an overflowing ashtray. Me and little dude hung then, watching Cartoon Network and talking about what the next school year would bring. Girls. Movies. Superheroes.

"Hey, Vig." He stared at the television, where a wolf and a pig smacked each other with hammers and put lit sticks of dynamite into each other's pants.

"Vig, buddy. Bedtime."

"Momma?"

"Sleeping. Come on. Let's get you in jammies."

Vig stared at the television as if I didn't even exist. I stood in front of him, and he tilted his body sideways so he could still see the flickering, blue-white pictures.

When I turned off the TV he cried, mad as the dickens, and turned his face to the wall and stuck his fingers in his mouth. I try to keep his nasty paws out of the maw, but when he's upset . . . well, there's no arguing with the little dude when he's tired.

He gave a soft little chuffing snore. I picked him up, carried him past snoring Moms, back to the bathroom, and put him on the pot so he wouldn't wet the bed. I don't think he even woke up on the pisser. He opened his eyes, smacked his lips just a bit, and let the yellow flow. It sounded loud in the stillness of the trailer.

Once he was down, I stepped outside and walked down to Coco's trailer. The light was on in her room, and her mom and dad had the television blaring at the trailer's other end. For folks who lived in Holly Pines Trailer Park, the Greens were well-off. Two newish cars and a doublewide without rats or cockroaches or holes in the linoleum where you could see the ground. Maybe that was just our trailer. I scratched on Coco's window.

I saw her shadow move behind the curtains, and she came over and raised the window.

"Shreve, what're you doing out this late?"

I shrugged. "Just got the kids to bed."

She gave a pained smile. "She bad tonight?"

"No worse than usual. Can I climb in?"

She paused and then shook her head. "I want you to, but . . . my dad would be furious if he caught you in here."

"It's been so long since we've hung out."

Her resolve cracked a little then. I kissed her and she kissed me back, over the windowsill, her soft lips meeting mine without reservation. But I felt other things in the kiss: nervousness, desire, fear, love. Maybe love. I don't know. It's amazing to me how you can know someone since you were a kid and love them with all your heart, and still not know if they love you back. Or even what they're thinking.

When we broke off, she said, “I’m sorry, Shreve. You can’t come in. But Dad’s going out of town next week on a contract job. Maybe then.”

“Okay. I understand.”

She ignored that, the self-pity. “How’s Vigor?” She always called him by his full name. She’s helped me put him to bed a hundred times if she’s done it once.

“Mad when I turned off the TV. But he settled down quick.”

“I miss him. Give him a kiss for me.”

I smiled. “Okay. Where is it?”

“Where’s what?”

“The kiss.”

She laughed softly. Then she leaned forward again, giving me a good one across the chops. I smelled her hair. She always smelled like fruit and perfume, but not sticky or too sweet. Powdery and light and clean.

As we kissed my mind flew away, out of my head and into the stars. Sometimes I imagined us married, with Vig as our son. I imagined us living happily in a big city, far away, where I worked in an office and she taught school and at night we ate dinner in a big kitchen, all three of us, laughing.

Off across the park, a gunshot sounded, someone cursed, and dogs began to bark. And for that instant I was furious—at my mother for being a drunk, at the world for the suck of gravity, at Coco’s father for keeping her from me. She pulled back, and all those emotions screwed themselves tight in a knot in my stomach and I did my best to smile at her again.

"Coco, I—"

"Sssh." She touched a finger to my lips. "I know. It's a monster of a world. It'll get better soon, Shreve. I know it will."

She kissed me again, let the curtain fall, and closed the window.

I walked back to my trailer and sat on the steps. The stars shone hard and bright overhead, indifferent to me.

Our trailer stood at the edge of the big piney woods—miles of needle-matted ground until you reached the old Rock Island Line tracks and then, a mile beyond that, the interstate. But behind me the glow of strip malls and pizza joints and gas stations and bowling alleys lit the sky and gave the edges of my vision a white halogen tint as I looked into the dark needles and trunks. I had a lighter in my pocket, for sparking Moms's smokes, and I took it out and flicked it, sending small tracers shooting away from my hands.

They say there are bear out there. I've seen raccoon, squirrel, and rabbits, possum (smeared across the highway), and deer. The numb-nuts in the trailer park are loaded for them all, with spotlights on trucks, gun racks in cabs, a rifle quick to hand in each trailer. At night you can always hear the crackle of gunfire, like popcorn, common and steady.

Sometimes I imaged burning it all down. All of it—the malls, the trailer park, the piney wood, everything. The fire would rise up to the heavens, and the smoke would choke out everything I know, blanket the world in white.

But there's the little dude to consider. Vig. Ferrous Vigor Cannon. Why'd she have to name him that?

▪▪▪

A big truck rumbled through the trailer park, and I knew who it was without seeing—fat Billy Cather, all double chins and chubby tires and jacked-up suspension and deer lights. The truck sounded like a freight train—or a tornado; take your pick in a trailer park—and lit up the night like a traveling circus. Cather pulled in two trailers down, and once he cut the engine I could hear the sounds of the radio—blaring electric guitars, heavy bass, and drums.

Cather stayed in there a long while, drinking beer, listening to the music.

There was a time when he was friendly with Moms and came by regularly. They'd drink and smoke, get loud and listen to her tape deck. He'd bring meat and grill out on the cement-block patio, and he'd tousle my hair and call me kiddo and hide his belches behind his hands. But one night they argued, I don't know about what, and then he stopped coming around. Which was fine with me.

When Cather finally got out of his truck, he swayed and staggered to his trailer door.

Late at night, in the park, when the drone of cars has fallen away, you can hear when someone coughs or goes to the bathroom, the trailer walls are so thin. I listened as Cather opened his fridge, farted like he was auditioning for first trumpet in a big band, popped a beer, stumbled back toward his bedroom, and turned on the TV.

I listened to the sounds of the park, the slamming of screen doors, televisions being switched off, the barking dogs quieting, settling down for the night. The cicadas whirred, their night chirrups rising and falling like strange waves washing a foreign shore. I watched the indifferent stars and followed a cloud bank moving glacially across the sky before I stood and walked slowly over to Cather's trailer and truck. His TV was loud, but as I approached the sound of his snores cut through the commercials hocking laundry detergent with scrubbing agents and whitening power.

I slowly opened the truck door and nearly ran when it pinged twice. Inside, beer cans littered the floorboard. I took all the change from the console, a flashlight, and some of the single dollar bills curled into a wad in the drink holder. There was a matte-black pistol, but I left that sitting there with the country music CDs. I was backing out of the cab when I saw the keys in the ignition.

I leaned back, out of the truck, to listen for Cather's snores. There weren't any. But the TV still blared, and I doubted anyone could hear me. The fatty probably shifted in his sleep and closed his mouth.

I stood there in the dark for a few long moments, thinking about the keys and the truck and my mom and Vig back in our trailer and how I'd never be able to leave until Vig was eighteen or Moms was dead, drowned in alcohol. And those keys said things to me that went beyond speech or even thought. Like maybe they were a jailer's keys, and all I had to do was turn them and change my life. Like there was nothing for it but to run.

I slipped behind the wheel and adjusted the seat, all without thinking. I cranked the ignition and the truck roared, vibrating and monstrous and raw. I threw it into gear, backed it out, yanking the wheel right so the truck's ass slewed left. And then I jammed it into drive and stomped the accelerator as far down as my foot would reach. The truck jumped and bucked like a bronco, the tail shifting and floating sideways, throwing the mud and gravel of the little trailer park road. Then finally the wheels caught and I was shooting forward, my heart doing its best to hammer its way out of my chest. And then the windshield went opaque with cracks, a million little facets, and I heard the cracks of what sounded like a rifle. Small pops, far away under the roar of the truck. And then the cab filled with a red fog, and I realized I was free, falling into the black, slipping into darkness, like a bird shot on the half-lit cusp where day meets night.

I looked down and saw the blood pumping from my arm, drenching my shirt and pants, making a crimson mess all over the cab. All I thought was that Cather would kill me if he caught me.

The truck slewed to the right. Now that I had trouble controlling it with my right hand, the steering wheel had a life of its own.

Then there were more pops, one after another. The front windshield collapsed, and the rear one as well, and I found myself in a shower of glass and furious wind. I thought I should crouch down to avoid being shot, but by then my body was as out of control as the truck. The rig slammed into a car, caromed off it, and sideswiped a trailer. And then I was spinning, upside down, on the ceiling of the cab, then on the floor, then slamming into the dashboard. I felt parts of me go crunchy inside, and I thought I might black out. But I never did; I never faded to black. I held on until the truck came to a stop, upside down, the engine still running.

I remember fat Cather's face filling the window, as angry as a devil's until he saw me. Then his face kinda crumpled like an empty beer can.

I'm sure I was quite a sight.

"Dammit. Dammit."

Mrs. Johnson appeared behind him, and her daughter. The girl had a cell phone to her ear and was speaking quickly to someone.

"It's the Cannon kid. The oldest." Mrs. Johnson covered her mouth and glared at Cather.

"He's been shot."

Cather sounded hurt. "I didn't mean to! He stole my truck! How was I supposed to know?"

"You just started shooting?"

Sirens sounded in the distance. Cather made a halfhearted effort to open the door and get me out.

"I'm sorry," I said. But the words didn't sound right, and Mrs. Johnson shushed me.

"Call again, Louise. He can't talk, and there's blood everywhere."

SEVEN

On the inside, on Saturdays Booth unlocks the remote controls for the televisions, each set hanging dead and dull behind chicken wire all week, and passes the remotes out to the boys with the least demerits—which, believe it or not, never includes me.

I tested it once and went on hiatus from the candy sales, did all my homework and towed the line, walked the straight and narrow, and didn't get one demerit all week. But when the time came to pass out the remotes, Booth looked at me, snorted, and said, "Shreve, I can't give this to you. If I did, you'll have bilked these kids out of their money before noon."

Idiot. I bilk them during the week. Saturday is my day off.

This Saturday I roll out of bed for headcount feeling good and looking forward to spending a little money at the commissary—which, on Saturdays, sells hamburgers and hot dogs and ice cream, Nutty Buddys, orange Push-Ups, and Rocket Pops. I plan on having one of each. I guess I'll buy Jack some too, since I'm flush and the little dude looks like he could use it.

Might as well be my day off—I can't compete with ice cream and the cold stuff anyway. It's a losing proposition.

Jack's bleary in the morning, wiping his eyes. I take my turn in the bathroom, run a hot shower, brush my teeth. On the line of my jaw is a pimple, a big nasty whitehead. Strange how popping it pleases me.

Sitting on his bed, Jack just looks around, blinking like he still can't believe he's in here, in the pokey, locked up with desperate and hardened juveniles thirsting for his blood. Yeah, right.

Maybe he's just not a morning guy. I hear him tossing and turning and calling out at night. He shakes my bunk when he sobs. Poor little dude.

Booth calls for headcount, and the wards clash and chatter, whooping and hollering and setting up basketball games for the free time we have in the yard today. Saturday is free day, and everyone is happy.

Except Jack. Jack's never happy. He just pretends he is.

"Jack. Come on, buddy, headcount."

I step out onto the walkway with a towel around my waist. There's more hooting and hollering, and someone whistles at me. I blow a kiss.

Jack comes to the walkway and assumes his position beside the door. We wait as Booth checks us off, and then we return to the semi-privacy of the cell. Jack lies back down on the bed. Sometimes in the morning, I'll find him under the bed, like it's a little fort and he's hiding. But in the day he's usually normal. Pretty normal. Okay, apparently normal.

I'm starting to worry about him.

"Listen, we got a free day. Why're you moping? I'm off work, no classes, extra-long yard time, the commissary is running, and the TVs will be on."

Jack's silent for a long while. Then he says, "The man is coming back today."

"Quincrux?"

"Yeah."

"Not today," I say. "It's Saturday."

Jack gives a little laugh. "So? Some folks work on Saturday, too. And Booth told me visitors come on Saturday."

This is true, and I tell Jack so. I never have visitors, but I see them when they get the tour. They're smiling but not enjoying themselves, seeing where their sons or brothers live, incarcerado.

"What's up with that guy? He's a perv or something."

I told Jack I had eavesdropped on his conversation with Quincrux. He nodded and smiled one of the few genuine smiles I'd ever gotten from him. Like he was touched I was looking out for him.

"All those weird questions . . ." Jack waves an absurdly over-fingered hand. "But he said he'll be coming back with a 'colleague.' I didn't like how that sounded."

To tell you the truth, I didn't either. I didn't like how any of Quincrux's talk sounded. When I think of Quincrux—his quiet, dead voice, his somber suit and briefcase, his bored, careless eyes—I feel cold and terrified. More terrified than when I thought I might bleed out and die.

I think about Quincrux a bit. I hold in my mind the jawbreaker that seemed to fend him off, to keep him out.

Jack stands, walks past the desk to the dresser and back. As he does I realize he hasn't ever settled in here. I've got posters plastering the walls. Dallas Cowboys and Razorback pennants. An 8x10 of Vig we took at the strip mall's Glamour Shots when he was a baby. Stacks of novels sent by the do-gooders at the sheriff's department outreach: King, Hemingway, Shelley, Howard. Hell, even Shakespeare. I'm not an idiot. I like to read. It makes the outside closer, the walls thinner. After a week, Jack's got his orange jumpers in a drawer, but no pictures of family, no posters of bands, no books, no magazines. And that reminds me that Quincrux left him a gift but I've never seen it. I never thought to ask.

"What was it Quincrux gave you? The gift that says something about you. And him."

Jack pulls a comic from underneath his mattress. "This. I meant to show you."

It's an X-Men comic. A big-breasted super-mutant with fiery eyes glares at me. Weird. She's hot but angry. What could make her so angry?

"I don't get it. What's he trying to say?"

Jack hesitates. He throws the comic onto the bed, then goes over to the desk and sits at the chair.

"I don't know." He sighs and looks down at his hands in his lap. "That I'm a mutant."

I laugh. "Naw. That's—I don't know—silly."

He looks at the door, making sure no one can see, and holds up his hand, fingers splayed.

"Not so silly."

"But it's just . . ." I stop and think a bit. I need to say this right. "My cousin is double-jointed. A kid I knew in school could add any two numbers in her head like lightning. You could just call 'em out, and she'd answer. You'd have to get a calculator to check, but she was always right. Another kid could play any instrument he could touch, like he'd been playing it all his life." This last one I saw on television, but I don't tell Jack that. "So I don't think having extra fingers makes you—"

"A mutant?" Jack shakes his head and sighs again. "It does make me different." He's not looking at me. He's got that far-off, thousand-mile stare. I worry that sometime the little dude won't be able to get back from wherever it is he goes when he gets that way.

"Hey, man. We're all different." That's what your momma believes. That we can all grow up to be president or millionaires and everyone is a little Van Gogh and there's never been another like us. But most kids in the general pop could be clones, all pressed out from the same mold, they're so damned homogeneous. Maybe I just think so because I don't know them well enough. But, I swear, all I have to get to know is one. But maybe Jack really is different.

"Let me buy you some ice cream, Jack, me boy. I'm flush this week and got a sweet tooth."

He laughs. "Awesome. I don't have any money."

"Heck, I'll even throw in a burger, son."

▪▪▪

We hit the commissary and eat the breakfast of champions: cheeseburgers, cheesy fries con jalapeños, and icy sodas, followed by orange Push-Ups. The Commons is a madhouse—the D-Wing cadre howling and throwing paper at the TV showing ESPN, and the C-Wing brutes glowering and gloating on the opposite side. Whoever holds the remote is king.

We head out to the yard, stomachs burbling.

Casimir Pulaski Detention Center is in the shape of a large X. A, B, C, and D wings form the arms of the cross, with Admin and classrooms and offices in the center, where the arms meet. The yard, a wide expanse of grass and basketball courts and bleachers lining a half-size football field, is one of the biggest differences between juvie and a penitentiary yard. The yard is lush, well-kept, and filled with balls and laughter and boys running about, acting like idiots, which is exactly the way boys are supposed to act.

Even I know that.

The illusion of a playground is broken only by the bulls. No Booth today. But Red Wolf, Wilkins, Peters, Blanchard, and Diegal lurk about, hands on billy clubs and pepper spray. We call the guards the League of Jerkwads. It's pretty obvious they want a general pop fight, but fights just don't happen that often ever since Big Paulie got shipped to the Farm.

All except Red Wolf. He doesn't want fights. He wants followers.

Red Wolf has a group of titty-babies on the smaller court, trying to teach them tribal dances. He ain't a real Indian, despite the fact he's holding court in full tribal garb, feathers and leathers and tomahawk and everything. He's a self-proclaimed phony Indian, which shouldn't make sense, but it does. He's bald, rail-thin, and polite to ward and guard alike. It's hard to tell how old he is.

I like him. He ain't Booth. He rolled up on me once, early in my career, when he was just dressed as a guard and not in some Indian costume. He's faster than he looks. He nabbed the sack with the sweets I was handing off, popped it open, then handed it over to the mark. He sniffed. "Ephemeral, boys. But your body is your body. You can pump all the junk in it you want."

In the yard, he moves through some prancing, horselike steps. The wards with him follow slowly, clumsily. They look at us, terrified, as we pass. Red Wolf waves at us and beckons, but I say to Jack, "Ignore him. He's trying to get them to transcend or find their totem animal or nonsense like that. He wants them to fly or something."

"Sounds fun."

Jack marches off toward the court and Red Wolf.

▪▪▪

"It not just your spirit, boys," Red Wolf says when we get close. "It's how your spirit is connected to your body and not connected to your body. We're all chained to our bodies, chained to the earth, incarcerado."

He turns to face the boys. He's in full Indian regalia: eagle feathers, leather with tassels, turquoise stuff I can't even recognize. But his baldness throws off the effect. He looks like a white man in a costume.

"I hear you boys say that, talking to each other. Incarcerado. Being locked up. But it doesn't mean that at all. You know what it means?"

The titty-babies look around sheepishly—at Red Wolf, at Jack, at me, then at themselves.

Jack says, "Meat? Like carne asada? Like . . . um . . . your body."

"No. But it's interesting you'd say that. You're locked into your own personal meat prison, when your spirit wants to fly. What's your name, son?"

"Jack. Jack Graves."

Part of me feels relieved not to be the object of a bull's attention. I'm glad Booth is gone and it's a Saturday and I'm not holding and there's nothing to worry about. Part of me is maybe just a bit jealous of the attention Red Wolf is giving Jack. But then I think of Quincrux and . . . well . . . then I'm cool with not getting all the attention.

Red Wolf turns to the other wards gathered on the basketball court. The sounds of basketballs dribbling, grunts, and catcalls from the other court fall away, and Red Wolf is there, in the center of it all, talking.

"They can lock up your body, but they can never lock up your spirit." He walks over to Raphael Santos, a meek little dude from two doors down on B Wing, and puts a finger on Raphael's chest. Red Wolf taps once, to make his point. "They can control your body." He raises his finger to Raphael's head and lightly, gently, puts his fingertip right in the center of Raphael's forehead. "They can't touch what's in here. Nothing can. What's in there can soar. Can rise up and shuck off this body, shuck off this detention center, and join with other spirits. It can ascend."

Red Wolf stops and bows his head. I want to laugh, it's such an obvious bit of theatrics. Red Wolf snaps back to us, turns around, doing the whole group eye-contact bit they must teach in church or college or wherever he learned it, and then claps his hands.

"This is the Ghost Dance. It's the dance that at one time all American Indian nations practiced, and it was inspired by an eclipse of the sun. It's the harbinger of the cleansing of the world." Red Wolf takes a prancing step, like a horse stomping, repeats it with the same foot, and then repeats the cycle with his other foot. He dances in a circle.

"Come on, boys. It's not hard. And when you do it, it separates your ghost, your spirit, from your body. Your body is incarcerado. But your spirit is free to roam. Roam now."

I look at Jack. He takes a step, then another with the same foot. And then we're all doing it, stomping around in circles on a basketball court in a kids' jailhouse named after a Pollock. If that isn't spirit-lifting, I don't know what is.

Jack's laughing now, an unreserved laugh that rises up toward the heavens, and I realize just how much he'd like to be freed from his body.

▪▪▪

When we come down, when we're back incarcerado, deep in our bodies, we walk out to where the grass rises to meet the chain-link fence topped with razor wire. We sit on the slope by the bleachers—the bleachers where I do a goodly portion of my deals. On a workday I take a seat, a mark walks below underneath the benches among the struts and trusses, tugs on my pants leg, and if I don't see the correct change appear on my bleacher, then no drop for the ravenous candymonger.

But today's my day off, so Jack and I sit in the sun to digest and watch the kids playing hoops—Ox, Reasoner, Fishkill, and a few goons from D Wing.

"So, you read that comic?" I'm leaning back on my elbows, watching the high, wispy clouds scuttle across the sky. "Any good?"

"Yeah. Storm gets some mutant kids that're being bullied and brings them to the school."

"Sweet. She's so hot. When did they start drawing her like that? Sometimes I wish they wouldn't."

Jack laughs, a real laugh, not an imitation of a real-boy laugh. He throws back his head, like when we did the

Ghost Dance, and lets his body go unguarded and at ease. I grin, resting on my elbows. I remember Vig and miss him horribly. Am I less tough to say that? Most likely I wasn't that tough to begin with. Just a talker with a way with the vocab. A salesman.

I feel good like I'd forgotten I could feel good, here with someone who needs me, not someone who wants something from me.

But Jack's laugh dies, quicker than I would have thought, and he's silent again, looking at the yard.

"You think he'll come today?"

He doesn't have to say who *he* is.

"Nah. It's Saturday. Even pervs like him need the afternoon off."

"Why do you keep calling him a perv?"

I have to remind myself that Jack's what? Twelve? Maybe thirteen? And been on the inside for just a week.

"Didn't you hear it? In his voice, when he asked about the . . . the diphallia." Someone with two penises.

At first I think Jack is embarrassed. It's hard talking to another guy about this stuff.

He's not embarrassed. He's furious.

The air in front of me dimples, wavers, like a boiling moat of water stands between him and me, sending up steam. I feel pressure on my shoulder, and then I'm toppling over and sliding away, down the hill, away from Jack.

"Jack! Stop!"

He slumps, coughs, and then begins to turn on the waterworks. It only takes a moment. I rise up on my hands and knees and climb back up to him.

Over and over again he's saying, "I'm sorry. I'm sorry."

I put my arm around him. He turns his face into his hands, just like Vig used to do when he was mad or ashamed.

"Jack, it's okay." I don't know what else to say. With Vig I could just make a goofy face or turn on the TV.

I don't know what's going on here, but I'm starting to understand why Quincrux is so interested in Jack.

"Hey, Shreve!" Reasoner yells. The basketball game is over. Ox, Reasoner, and the rest of them stand at the bottom of the slope, looking up at us. "You getting sweet on the fish?"

I shoot him the bird, just to let him see what I think of him.

One of the D goons says, "Let's see him do that, so we can get a load of the fingers."

I look at Ox, and he's patently not looking at me. He's doing whatever he can to not look at me. The rest of the guys walk up the slope. Fishkill looks like he wants to kill me for shooting him the bird. Reasoner's grinning his goofy, yellow-toothed grin, happy there's game afoot.

"You told." Jack's old voice is back, dead and hollow. And grim as the reaper.

"I . . . I didn't mean . . ."

What can I say? I told. Whatever my intentions, I told.

"I had to get Ox to let me in his room. He promised . . ."

The boys stand in front of us now. Jack stands too, slowly, his hands in fists at his side.

"Back up," Jack says. There's iron there.

Ox snorts and Reasoner laughs, making a phlegmy, grotesque sound. The D-Wing goons start moving around to Jack's sides.

On the inside, pack mentality rules the yard. I've said it before, and I will say it again: Everyone thinks he's different. But when you truly are different, the difference gets beat out of you on the yard. I don't have to be a mind reader to know things are about to get bloody.

"Step away, Shreve. We just want to see the freak show."

"No." I've fought before. I've lost. Why do you think I love words? "Listen, boys. You do this, you're off the client list. No more of the sweet stuff for any of you."

The largest D goon says, "You don't sell it to us anyways, you stuck-up little dick." If this were a cartoon, he'd be cracking his knuckles right now. But he doesn't. He just stands there.

"We just want to see the hands." Reasoner's looking at Jack. Jack stares back, stone-faced and defiant.

"No," he says. And the air around him begins to waver.

Something's about to happen.

The tension I felt building when I listened through Ox's vent is in the air again. The air is ripe with storm, with electricity or ozone or smoke or something, something destructive, and I can't know what it will be until it happens. But it will happen, and soon.

Reasoner steps in close, and the D-Wing goon follows. His feet are spaced wide and his elbows pulled in tight with his fists balled, like he's a kung-fu master or an action figure.

"What's going on here, boys?" Booth. And I didn't even hear the jangle of keys. He's standing right behind Ox.

All of the sudden the circle of brutes evaporates. Reasoner runs toward the bleachers, yelling over his shoulder, "Nothing!"

The Kung-Fu Master says, "Catch you later, Shreve, Fingers."

Ox shambles off, head down. He's an overfed ox that's just been shocked. Or maybe neutered. The big lug feels bad about spilling the beans. Still. No more candy for him. Though, without his protection, I just might be out of the candy-dealing business.

Like it or not, Jack Graves has changed my life.

When they're gone, I can see Quincrux standing at the bottom of the slope, just to the left of the bleachers. So that's why Booth was looking for us—for Jack. Quincrux is holding his briefcase and wearing a black suit and fedora, like he's a G-man from a black-and-white movie. Beside him stands a woman. She's short and shaped like a dumpling, with gigantic matronly breasts straining the seams on a business suit as severe as Quincrux's. Her hair is hideous. She has bangs like a Romulan, with chunky side curls that make her look like a doll some child has taken lawn shears to.

Booth glowers at us. "Answer me, Shreve. What in the world is going on? Is this your attempt at gang war or something?"

I'm really not in the mood for Booth's nonsense. "Yeah, it's me and Jack against all of general pop, Booth. They don't stand a chance."

Booth throws up his hands. "I'd like you better, Shreve, if you could just answer a question straight for once."

"How's this? Those jerks were getting ready to pounce on us."

"Why?"

Quincrux, from behind Booth, says, "Why, indeed, Mr. Cannon?"

I can't explain it, but for a moment I'm afraid when I realize he knows my name.

"Reindeer games."

"Ah. A comedian." Quincrux sounds bored. Like everything is tiresome, deathly tiresome, and he'd be as happy to see me dead as deal with me.

Booth, turning, says to Quincrux, "You won't get anywhere with this one, Mister—"

Booth shudders like he's been punched. He goes slack but doesn't fall. He turns back to us slowly, too slowly. Booth loves his clothes, his neatly combed hair, his pencil-thin mustache. He holds himself like a rooster, chest out, hands on his hips, resting on his cuffs, his mace, his zip ties, ready to subdue any unruly ward of the state he happens to encounter. He's an idiot, but he's a predictable idiot. But now his body has changed. His shoulders slump. His face, normally angry or gleeful or annoyed when he sees me, is blank. His arms hang loose by his side. Without the bluster, he seems small, fragile. I might not like the everyday Booth, but the empty one—the vacant Booth—I like even less.

"Now that we're alone," Quincrux says, slow and deliberate, "Ilsa, if you would take care of Mr. Graves, I will address Mr. Cannon."

"Wait!" I don't know what else to do. "What do you want with Jack?"

The woman approaches with little mincing steps, as though she were on the dance floor. She's nearly popping out of her skirt, so maybe her clothes are too tight to let her walk. Or maybe she's full of herself.

She makes a sound like mmmmm, as though she's just found a turkey leg where she least expected it.

"The arrogant one." She's looking in my direction. "He looks much more appetizing. I like the gristle." She's got an accent. German or something.

Quincrux frowns. "Unfortunately, Ilsa, I think you're mistaking obstinacy for arrogance. However, there will be no . . . no dining. Is that clear?"

"Yes, Quin," she says. She smiles, showing more teeth than I think is humanly possible. She's got a mouthful of chompers. None look too sharp. None look too dull, either.

"We're not going with you," I say.

Quincrux looks around at the fences and walls and holds his hand upward, as though feeling for rain. "Where might you go, Mr. Cannon? It seems your defiance might be a bit misguided." He steps closer, and now a grim look is on his face. He's through playing around.

"Ilsa, please secure Mr. Graves, and I'll see to young master Cannon."

The air becomes tense, and then my head splits open like I've been axe-struck. Something . . . no, someone is trying to get in. The sun dims. The sounds of boys playing on sun-warmed dirt and concrete, the smell of grass, the feel of wind on my skin, the dust from the yard—they all diminish and fade. They're gone and replaced with the pain and the insistent pressure on my mind, like a snake trying to hatch from an egg, but backward, in reverse—a snake trying to re-enter the egg. To be unborn.

I don't know what to do. I can't think, and there's only panic left. My head screams with pain, and then I realize it's not my head screaming. I've dropped to my knees, and I'm screaming like a child stung by a wasp.

I remember in the cafeteria, when Quincrux took my thoughts. He lured them out and away. I've been trying to forget that, I think, this whole time. But now he's doing more than that. He's the wolf at the door, blowing down the house, sniffing to get in.

I fight. I try and make the surface of my thoughts as hard as diamond and as slick as greased steel.

I picture a sphere. Hard and strong and unbreakable.

A jawbreaker.

Through the pain, I feel Quincrux's rage. He's not bored now. He wants in, the wolf, and all that's in his way is the jawbreaker. He can crunch the jawbreaker, he can gnash, but his teeth will break before it does. He's huffing and puffing at the door, and soon he'll want to blow the house down.

I guess this makes me the little piggy.

The pressure stops.

Quincrux chuckles. "He's more than gristle, Ilsa. But no matter. Round one is over, Mr. Cannon. And round two will tell all."

In the time I have, I glance at Jack. He's shuddering, a pained look on his face. His hands are out, all twelve fingers splayed. His eyes are locked on the woman.

Quincrux invades again. An assault of unimaginable strength. His mind isn't a single snake, but a multitude of serpents with noses like needles. They're looking for some crack, some crevice to slip inside. To penetrate. I hold the jawbreaker in my mind. I hold it until it becomes me, my spirit, like I've performed the Ghost Dance and shucked off my body. I'm no longer incarcerado. But the serpent heads become teeth. Great gnashing teeth.

The jawbreaker shatters, and Quincrux is in.

I'm pushed back and away from myself, as if I were looking down from some great height at my body.

I'm not screaming anymore. I stand, even though I don't will myself to. I'm not running this rodeo anymore—

someone else holds the reins. Quincrux. He's more than riding me. He's inside me, wearing me like a Sunday suit. I still perceive, but I'm just a passenger.

I'm happy to see Quincrux didn't get in without a little effort. His nose streams with blood, and his face is pale, chalky.

Pulling a handkerchief, he looks at the woman, wipes his nose, and says, "I have him secure. The other boy?"

"What took you so long, dear Quin?" She's gloating. "This one didn't even put up a real fight."

"Ah, Ilsa. You truly are a wonder. Your handling of supernumeraries is, as I've told you many times before, laudable. It seems your ability to penetrate them has saved us again." Quincrux tucks his bloody handkerchief in his pocket. "Which is why you are here, since I am recovering from the incident in Maryland."

"Ah. You were always the strong one, dear. I would have never thought this child could best you."

"It's not a matter of besting. It's a matter of recovery. And I am not yet whole. Had I been, I could make this entire yard of boys kill each other. Gleefully."

When Quincrux says *gleefully*, I can't tell whether he's referring to himself or how he'd make us all kill one another. If I had a body, I would shudder.

"Doubtful." Ilsa sniffs as though wounded. "I can make five my slaves. But more than that, it's impossible to maintain control."

"You lack imagination. It can be done, but not without

a little sacrifice." The inflection when Quincrux says *sacrifice* goes beyond his bored, now tired, expression.

"What happened in Maryland that could have left you so weakened?"

Jack walks up next to where I stand, and together, almost in time, we approach Booth. Like little windup soldiers, the three of us march toward the door that leads back inside Casimir. Quincrux and the woman follow behind. Ox, Reasoner, and the goons watch from the basketball courts. What they wanted to do to us . . . I'd prefer that now.

"There are things, Ilsa, that are better not to know. What lives in Maryland is beyond my ken. Beyond your ken. It is off-limits. And I advise you not to probe there for fear of your life."

I have no idea what Quincrux and Ilsa are talking about. I don't want to know.

With Booth accompanying us, they take us back to our room, sit us on the bed, and begin their examination.

EIGHT

On the inside, when I had control of myself, the world seemed never-changing. There's a comforting permanence to prison. To juvie. But now, on the outside looking in, everything looks desperate, mutable. I realize, like Moms in our trailer, I'm just a tenant in a meatsuit, liable to be evicted at any time.

Ilsa licks her chops and looks at me.

"Never mind the boy," Quincrux says. "Release Mr. Graves so that he and I might converse."

Jack gasps and then falls over, like a puppet with its strings cut. He shivers on the floor.

"When you are ready, Mr. Graves, we will require you to disrobe so that we may examine your whole body. Your hands and feet are interesting, but we need to see just how different you are."

The perv is still interested in Jack's junk.

"Give him a prod, Ilsa."

"I'll just make him disrobe."

"I prefer capitulation. It makes the interview go that much easier in the end."

Jack sits upright. "No."

"That is your choice." Quincrux shifts in the chair and adjusts my notebook on the desk. "However, let me warn you, if you resist, I'll snuff out your friend's mind like extinguishing a candle. If you care for him at all, you'll do as I say."

I'm sorry I told Ox about your fingers, Jack. Jack stands and takes off his clothes. No diphallia. Nothing else out of the ordinary other than he could use some fattening up. His ribs are clearly visible.

Quincrux looks disappointed. Ilsa sniffs as though looking at an empty plate.

"Another goose chase, eh, Quin? All this effort on these . . . these human wastes of space."

Quincrux tsks, withdraws a pressed white handkerchief and wipes his hands. "Put on your clothes, boy."

Jack begins pulling on his underwear.

"Can I have the tough one?" Ilsa asks, and her voice sounds hungry and childish all at once.

Quincrux pauses, thinking. "I don't think that would be wise, dear. He interests me a bit. He put up more of a fight than you'd expect of a normal delinquent."

"All the more reason to dispose of him."

"No." Quincrux is curt, and I realize his dead, bored tone has been gone since he took control of my body. "I don't want to alarm the authorities. This one," he jerks a thumb at Booth, "is beginning to question his memory loss. Do we wipe him, too? I think not."

"All right, then. You are," she clears her throat, "the boss."

"I need to ask a few more questions."

"Go ahead, dear. I have time." Damn me if she doesn't rummage through her purse and withdraw a needlepoint pattern and thread. It's probably a picture of a ham.

Once Jack is dressed, he sits down on the bed, looking scared. I've seen Jack angry now, and sad, but I've never seen him this cowed. He's a tough little dude, too, this Jack is. But now he looks defeated.

"What happened to your parents, Jack?"

"They died."

"How?"

"An explosion."

"How is it that you survived?"

"I don't know. I was three then."

Quincrux nods, and rubs his chin.

"The incident at the foster home. What happened?"

"They were going to beat me up, the older kids."

"Did they?"

"No."

"What happened?"

"I don't remember."

"Did you fight them?"

"Yes."

"And . . ."

"I won, I guess."

"How is it a boy your age, a child of thirteen—an undersized boy, I might add—could defeat five older children in hand-to-hand combat?"

"I don't know. Why did your nose start bleeding?"

"Ah. You still have some backbone left."

Suddenly I'm back in my body, and my head is full of pain. I cry out. I scream. Then, before you can say diphallia, I'm kicked out again.

Jack looks at my body with wide eyes and a tear-streaked face.

Quincrux says, "He put up a fight, your friend. But I won. I would advise you to remember this. Why were you so different with similar odds?"

"I don't know."

"Ilsa?"

"He's telling the truth. There's been no lying as far as I can tell. But he's guarded. There can be no mistaking this."

"Is it possible he doesn't understand his own powers?"

"Doubtful. He knows he's different, but it has to do with his hands. They're a mark of shame to him." She huffs, and rests her needlepoint on her massive breast. "A goose chase, I say."

"Sometimes, Ilsa, I think you want us to fail."

She says nothing, but clucks in her throat. She pulls a needle through the pattern, tugs the thread, then makes another pass.

Quincrux stands, smooths his slacks, picks up his absurd fedora, and places it on his head.

"You will forget this, Mr. Cannon. I command it. Ilsa?"

"This one will remember nothing other than an absolutely beautiful woman and kind man from the state, inquiring after his welfare."

"Are you sure?"

"Of course, darling. Of course."

Quincrux shrugs, picks up his briefcase, and moves toward the door. He puts his free hand on Booth's shoulder, lightly, the way a friend might.

"Thank you for your hospitality, Mr. Booth. Once again, you have been very accommodating. Very accommodating."

Booth shudders, looks around, and blinks. He doesn't respond. He stumbles over to the chair Quincrux just vacated. His nose begins to bleed, messing up his perfect pencil-thin mustache. Poor Booth.

Ilsa stands and looks at me. Suddenly I realize I'm back inside my own head, looking out of my own eyes, with a splitting headache. On her way past, she hands me a tissue.

She pats my cheek. "Delicious boy. Your nose is bleeding."

She winks as they leave.

Booth says, "What just happened?"

Nothing.

Nothing just happened.

▪▪▪

Quincrux can "command" all he wants, but I know what I know. The next time I see him and the witch, I'll kill them and earn my place incarcerado. As God is my witness, I will.

Jack's a different matter. He can't remember anything past the Ghost Dance.

"Nothing? You don't remember anything?"

"No. I remember a beautiful woman and—"

"Jesus H. She wasn't beautiful. She had pockmarks and was shaped like a fatted hog."

"Oh." He remains quiet for a few moments. Then he looks up and holds up his hand, showing me his fingers. "I don't know what to believe. Everything. Nothing." He sighs and makes a fist. He's skinny, but his fist looks fat with all those extra fingers. "I believe you, Shreve. I do. It's just . . ."

"Just what?"

"I can't remember. Any of it."

Giving him all the story takes a while. I think I remember everything those monsters said. But Jack? Nada.

After all is said and done, I say, "I don't think Booth can remember, either."

"Why can you when we can't?"

"Maybe I'm different."

Jack smiles at the irony of that and looks down at his hands.

The smile means a lot to me. I feel terrible for telling Ox about Jack's hands. They'll be coming for us, the meaner denizens of Casimir. And I'm starting to get an idea of Jack's defenses.

His smile fades, and he puts his hands between his knees. He doesn't look at me, just rolls over on his bunk to face the wall. It's like we're back to the beginning.

When I talk to him, he won't answer. Silence is something I'm getting used to.

NINE

On the inside, Sundays are a cakewalk for the pious. Priests, reverends, ministers, and evangelists crowd into the hallways of Casimir Pulaski and invade the classrooms with punch and casseroles and pamphlets. There's the Catholics and the Episcopalians in the penguin suits. The Methodists, Presbyterians, and Lutherans in their cheap blazers and Wal-Mart slacks and penny loafers. And then there are the Baptists in their chicken-fried getups: skinny ties and snakeskin boots. The Baptists are like salesmen or beggars—you can't make eye contact or they'll start preaching. They don't bring anything inside Casimir except Bibles and the heat of their faith.

A Nation of Islam guy came for a while, but Warden Anderson doesn't have much liking for anything un-Christian and ran him off. He was kind of cool. He just sat while all the other ministers scurried around preaching or serving chicken spaghetti casserole. He'd listen to his headphones and read the Quran. He had a sign around his neck that said, "Ask." And we did. We wanted to know what he was all about.

The Warden didn't like that. Pass revoked.

But God? Salvation? Damnation? I don't believe in any of that. Yeah, there might be a god. Yeah, we all might be something more than atoms bouncing off one another. But if there's some bearded bean counter in the sky, he doesn't care about us. Otherwise, kids wouldn't die. There'd be no cancer. There'd be no bastards. No one would ever have a drunk for a mother. Or sprout extra fingers where no fingers are supposed to grow.

No. He don't care about us.

▪▪▪

Jack's quiet today. We walk through Commons, through the general pop, and it, too, is quieter than usual for a Sunday. There's pressure on my back, and it's coming from the heavy eyeballing the wards of the state currently give us. You can feel it, the pressure—there's physics to it, like the speed of light or the weight of gravity. It's palpable. It's there.

It doesn't take a mind reader to know this is all because of my fat mouth. Words are my thing. Words are what they'll put on my tombstone.

A cluster of D-Wing goons whistle and make fish faces at Jack, who hunches his shoulders and stuffs his hands deeper into his pockets. Someone yells, "Hey, Fingers! Give us the bird!"

Sounds like Kenny or Reasoner, but I can't be sure. They're both hoarse little ratfinks. I give them two birds. Then I spot Booth, arms crossed over his chest, standing under the chicken-wire television. It's in the rulebook that rude gestures warrant detentions, but he doesn't do anything. Enemies are required to do their best. Why doesn't he do something? He just watches as Jack and I run the general pop gauntlet. We walk through the doors into the cafeteria and down the wide hallway until we find the right classroom.

A man unwraps aluminum dishes and sets out paper plates and Dixie cups.

"Hey, padre!" I greet the man and point at Jack. "Father Glick, meet Jack Graves. He's new."

The man straightens from where he's arranging aluminum trays. He sees me, smiles, and says, "Shreve. How many times do I have to tell you, I'm just a layperson, a member of the vestry? No need to call me Father."

I ignore him and take a peek at the spread.

The penguins got wise and realized the wards would stick around for the hard sell as long as there was grub. Today there's cheese grits, cheese enchiladas, and cheese dip. If Glick could figure out a way to get cheese in the tea, there'd be some cheesy tea up in Casimir. That's for damned sure.

He's from the Episcopal camp, which means he wants to be hip and young and accessible to our special situations. But he still reads from a Bible or liturgy or the inspirational tracts and self-help books he always brings with him.

I'm fine with a little proselytizing because I'm quite partial to enchiladas. And Mrs. Glick makes some mean ones, she does. Were she not such a fantastic cook, I might not be as open to the ferv.

Jack follows me to the tucker. Another couple kids from A Wing are there already, with paper plates full of chips and cheese dip and Dixie cups of sweet tea.

"Help yourselves to the food. Please, if you have any allergies, read the sheet there"—he points to a computer printout—"and make sure that you'll be okay eating this offering."

We pile our Dixie plates high with the goods, grab plastic cutlery and sweet tea, and take seats near the back of the classroom, where we can keep our backs to the wall and face the door. Back here the light comes in through the big barred windows, and you can see out over the razor wire and into the trees and the neighborhood beyond where cars drive by and kids play in yards and have parents who give a shit about them.

We dig in. Jack's a weird kid, all right—fingers everywhere, thin as a whip, and somber as a mortician. But it looks like he enjoys Mexican food.

We eat and watch the kids wander in and out of the classroom. Some glance at us. Father Glick stands at the front of the class and begins to sermonize. I don't listen. I look right at him as he stands up there and speaks of Jesus, and I don't let a single thing he says enter my perception. I smile and eat and drink. I watch the kids coming in and out of the classroom. Some stop and listen to Father G. Some stop and get food.

When the sermonizing comes to an end, Father G walks back and gives us pamphlets and says, "I hope you'll come to St. Mark's when your stay here is over. We always welcome new members to the church." I smile and thank him. This guy is the real deal, a believer. He wants the best for his fellow man, and he includes both me and Jack in that number. Part of me wishes I could buy into his wonderful little dream full of martyrs and enchiladas and tortilla chips with queso. But Vig is still gone and Moms is still drunk and Jack still has too many fingers on his hands and there are still monsters in human skin out in the world wanting to eat kids like me. So, Father Glick is a nice guy. But a blind one.

He starts putting aluminum foil back on the dishes and gets a cart and loads all the remains of the food. No more kids come walking in and out of the classroom. Jack and I sit in the spill of light from the window.

The sky is a watery blue, and thin, wispy clouds obscure the autumn sun.

"You think we're in for it, Shreve?" Jack's looking at me straight. Not looking at his hands, not mumbling. Just asking an unvarnished question. "The guys in Commons seemed like they wanted to kill me."

I sigh. It's a hard truth I have to tell.

"Yeah. We're in for it, one way or another. We're all in for it, eventually."

The sun comes out from behind the slight clouds, the light grows, and I turn my face up to it and close my eyes.

"Thing is, Jack, it isn't any different in here than it is out there, beyond the fence. They find out you're different, they want to know how different you are."

I open my eyes. He stares at me, unblinking, quiet and motionless in that way he has. Then he nods.

We sit in the spill of light. Motes hang suspended in the air, swirling lazily, and it's easy to drift off with our stomachs full, looking at the bright sky.

"What do you want with your life, Shreve?"

That's out of left field, as the saying goes.

"I don't know. My brother. To make sure he's okay and isn't totally screwed up by my mom." I smile, cross my arms behind my head. "I want to see my girlfriend, I guess."

"What about your dad?"

"What about him?"

"Is he—?"

"Don't know if he's alive or what. He's a nobody. A never-was."

He's quiet for a while, thinking about it. His parents died. My parents ignored and abandoned me. Never knew I existed, maybe. Hard to say which is worse.

"You've got a girlfriend?"

"I did . . ." My turn to think about things. "Probably not anymore."

"What's her name?"

"Coco."

He nods again, like he's storing away that information.

"So, what do you want, Jack? What do you want out of life?"

He doesn't hesitate. "What I'll never be able to have." He looks down at his hands—his damned hands. Always the reminder. "I want to be normal. I want to fit in."

"Why?"

"I . . ." He's taken aback by the question. "So I don't hurt anyone."

"How do they get hurt?" I think I know, but I don't think he does. "What happened to you?"

Jack's still as only he can be. Eventually he opens his mouth. Then he closes it, like a fish out of water.

Finally, he says, "I killed them."

"Who?"

"My parents."

"No. How? How could you have done that?"

"I don't know. Just, when I'm scared or . . . angry . . . things happen."

"Like the Hulk."

He nods and gives a choked laugh, and wipes the tear that's come to his eye. It's a laugh full of self-disgust and hopelessness. My heart breaks to hear it. If I heard that come from Vig . . . I don't know what I'd do.

Jack keeps going. He's started, and now he can't stop. "I was three. And I remember waking from a horrible dream to find the house burning around me, and flashing lights." He stops, puts his face in his hands. "I don't even remember what they looked like.

"They said it was a gas leak. A miracle I survived. I had no other family, no one who'd take me in. So they put me in a foster home. That was . . . years ago. I've slept on every kind of floor, you know. In sleeping bags and closets and on cots. I've gone from family to family. And always, something goes wrong and I'm sent somewhere else. Until now." He looks around at the classroom, at the windows, the bars dividing the light pouring in from the frigid sky. He stares at me.

"Shreve . . . I . . ." He squares his shoulders. "I don't want you as my friend. I can't . . . It just won't work. Everyone who gets near me ends up hurt. I'm sure Booth or the Warden will move me into another cell—"

"Bullshit." It comes out of me before I know what I'm saying. "You might not want me as your friend. Fine. But you can't stop me from being yours. You can't pick your family, they say. Well, you can't pick your friends either. Or get rid of me so easy. And I'm alert. I know. Maybe even more than you."

"What do you know?"

"What happens."

"What happens?"

"Yeah."

There's a noise from the front of the room, and at first I think it's more kids looking for enchiladas. But then in walks Reasoner, smiling triumphantly. Ox trails along behind.

"There he is, boys. Fingers and his girlfriend."

Looks like we're having a party and we were the last to know. The Kung-Fu Master hops into the room, and Fishkill follows after.

They spread out.

"We wanted to finish our little talk from the yard, gents." The Kung-Fu Master looks at Reasoner and then dusts his hands off on his jumpsuit. "No big deal. We just wanna check out the freak show."

Jack's standing now, his desk kicked away. The look on his face isn't one I'm likely to forget soon. It's hard and careless. Fierce. He looks like he could kill.

Oh, no.

I remember the way he spoke to Quincrux, both of their dead voices. Quincrux laconic and bored, and Jack puzzled but numb. I think he just stopped caring whether he hurts somebody. Just a word, and that switch was thrown.

Jack takes two steps toward the other boys.

"Hoss, I think you better get your little buddies out of here," I say to Ox. "Something's gonna happen."

Ox's brow furrows, drawing down into a big, hairy V. God, he's a freaking animal, he is.

"I told you not to call me that, Shreve."

Kung-Fu Master and Fishkill move to our sides, and Ox comes in closer, so that most of us are in the middle of the desks. But Ox isn't focused on Jack. He's bristling with anger and looking at me.

"Yeah? You told me not to call you hoss, hoss? That it?"

Fishkill looks at Ox and says, "Stop messing with Shreve, man. I just want to see the weirdo." Fishkill turns back to Jack. "Come on, man. We don't want to hurt you. We just want to check out the fingers."

"No." Jack's voice sounds tight and unafraid. I don't think he's even aware of me anymore. I've got to keep them off him. For their own good.

"Hey, hoss, Fishkill holding your leash now? At least I fed you. I know how to keep barn animals happy."

It's a thousand pounds, I think, the load of bricks that lands on my face. A thousand pounds of brick and stone, wrapped in meat. I fall backward into the desks, scattering them.

When I stop skidding and hitting chair legs with my body and come to a rest in a tangle of metal desks, when my head stops spinning and the pulsing alien thing now living in the flesh of my cheek calms enough for me to rise up on my elbows, I point my throbbing head in the direction of where I was just standing, next to Jack, before the thousand pounds hit my face.

For a beast of burden, Ox is fast.

He's coming toward me, taking big steps, hands balled into fists. The floor needs more mopping, it seems.

Beyond him, I see Jack surrounded by Fishkill, Reasoner—still grinning his malicious little grin—and the Kung-Fu Master.

"Come on, freak. Give us a look. Show us the hands."

The air around Jack ripples now. And that tension, the

invisible pressure, builds. My ears pop.

Ox kneels in front of me, blocking my view of Jack. He snatches my jumpsuit at the neck and hoists me from the floor.

"This is a mistake, hoss. You're gonna regret it—"

"Shut your mouth. I'm not your dog."

"No, that'd be an insult to all dogs—"

You'd think it wouldn't hurt so much this time. But pain, it can constantly reinvent itself. And this time Ox just slaps me. It's not a normal slap. It's a slap bred from toffee, chocolate, and pure vitriol. It's a slap that freaking animal was born to give. It lands on the side of my head and knocks my whole body sideways, but the brute holds me in place. I feel like I've just been in a car wreck.

I open my mouth, because that's what I do. I talk; I talk, and words are my thing. But now there's no air to breathe. My mouth's full of blood, and Ox has slammed his massive ham-hock of a fist into my stomach, so all the choice insults I was going to sling at him, spit at him, sting him with—all the vile insults I was going to use to hurt his delicate ego—they'll all have to wait until later. When I can breathe.

I slump to the floor. Blood flows from my nose and pools from my lips. My lungs aren't working.

From where I lie, I see Jack surrounded by the other boys. His body is rigid, held so immobile he looks like a little statue. *The Angry Kid* is what they'd call it, I think, if it were a statue.

"Come on, freak. Show us the hands, or Ox here is gonna have to do you like he did Shreve."

Everything slows. It feels like I've dived to the bottom of the deep end of a swimming pool and my ears are just about to collapse from the water pressure.

And then Ox steps near, Reasoner raises his hands to grab Jack's bicep, and the air wavers horribly, like it was gelatin or dimpled glass. Now Reasoner's and Fishkill's eyes open wide in surprise, and Ox—the gigantic stupid animal—raises his arms.

Jack shows them his hands.

He throws them out like he's slapping glass.

The air explodes.

An invisible wall slams into me, ripping at my hair and clothes. Desks scatter in front of the shockwave, rocketing outward and away. The last thing I see before passing out are the goons flying backward and Ox toppling toward me.

And Jack. Jack standing at the center of a circle of destruction.

▪▪▪

I'm not out long, I don't think. Reasoner groans from the far wall, and Ox is breathing. He's halfway on top of me, his massive trunk across my legs. Kung-Fu and Fishkill are down and indeterminate.

Jack stands over me, wringing his hands. My grandmother used to do that. She wasn't as dangerous as Jack, except when she sneaked smokes by her oxygen tank. Luckily, when she exploded she only took herself and the trailer.

"Shreve, you okay? I'm sorry—"

"Shut up." I spit a blood loogey onto the floor. I push myself up but don't move. I try again. "Help pull this moron off me."

"Oh . . . no. Shreve, I'm so—"

"Shut up."

I don't really feel like hearing the apologies right now. And hell, he doesn't need to apologize to me anyway. We wouldn't be here if it wasn't for my mouth.

Between the two of us we move the side of beef off my legs, and Jack pulls me up. My head throbs. Blood drips from my nose, trickles down the back of my throat, wells in my mouth. It feels like someone is dribbling a basketball on my face where Ox hit me.

I'm thinking that Ox did more damage to me than Jack's . . . talent. Special gift. Curse. Whatever.

When I'm standing, I grab Jack's arm and lean into him.

"See? You can't get rid of me that easily." I cough and spit a huge wad of gore onto Ox's chest. "Let's go. We've got to clear out."

Before we go, I check pulses. Reasoner's moaning. Kung-Fu is bleeding pretty bad where a desk edge caught his leg. He could be in bad shape, really. But he deserves it.

On the way out I pull the fire alarm so these assholes don't die. With Jack helping me, we make it out of the classrooms and into Commons before the guards arrive.

We duck into the Commons bathroom, surprising the titty-babies there getting shook down by a couple of oxymorons. When they see the blood streaming from my face, they stop their reindeer games and vacate.

We clean up my cheek as best we can. Jack brings me paper towels to wipe the gore, but there's nothing we can do about the side of my kisser. It's swollen to twice its normal size and beginning to discolor. It feels as bad as it looks.

I look like the Elephant Man.

"Gotta get back to the room, Jack."

"Okay."

"We're gonna have to split, you realize?"

"Yeah, we can't stay here."

"I don't mean the bathroom. Split here. Casimir."

Jack's eyes widen just a little, but he understands.

"Quincrux."

"Yeah. When he gets wind of this, he'll be back. And the witch will be with him."

Jack looks puzzled. The witch really must have scrambled his noggin good. He can't remember.

"It doesn't matter if you can't remember her. Quincrux is bad enough by himself. And this time he won't be content with asking you to move glasses of water. He'll take you away to . . . to . . . wherever."

Jack sighs, squares his shoulders, and says, "I'm tired of moving."

"Nothing for it except to run. You believe that?"

He looks at me, face-to-face, and nods. "Yeah. I guess

so. I remember the man."

I hold out my hand, like I've done a million times with Vig, for him to slap. To give some skin. But Jack just puts his hand in mine, as if to shake. I look down at the over-fingered hand in my mitt, cover it up with my other hand so I'm giving the politician's pump, and smile.

"This is nothing," I say, meaning his extra fingers, or his explosive ability, or even his strangeness. Or maybe I mean the fact we're incarcerado. Or my mangled face. I mean it all, maybe. Or nothing. I don't know.

But maybe Jack understands what I'm trying to say.

"We stick together." That's pretty clear, even with my throbbing head. "So let's go back to the cell. Stay between me and Norman. Right? Otherwise, he'll see . . ." I point at the pulsing balloon that's the side of my face.

I feel dizzy for a moment and catch myself on the sink before I fall. Ox messed me up good. I'd like to pay him back . . . but . . . I guess I had it coming. I rode him too hard.

▪▪▪

Nothing happens. We walk past Sloe-Eyed Norman with no problem. He presses the button that opens our cell door, and it swings wide and stays that way—no closed doors on the wing during daylight hours with wards inside.

Once we're back in the room, I lie on Jack's bunk. I can't manage to climb into mine.

"Your face looks horrible."

"Thanks. And you're a beauty, too."

When I giggle, remembering Reasoner's expression right before Jack blew up, the movement sends shooting pains through my face, but damn . . . I don't even care. Thank god I'm as abrasive as I am, otherwise I might have never figured out our twelve-fingered boy was a time-bomb. A walking timebomb.

Jack pads into the bathroom. I hear the water run, and when he returns he's got a hand towel dripping with water. It feels like ice when he puts it on my cheek.

What a guy.

Once the towel warms, I say, "Listen, Jack. Can you do your explodey trick without . . . I don't know . . . getting angry?"

Jack's reaching for the towel and stops. He cocks his head.

"What do you mean?"

"Jack, the explosion. The shockwave that came from you. Don't you remember?"

Jack's looking at me but not seeing me. His eyes are going back and forth in their sockets, moving over a mind's-eye scene. Now they grow wider, and he drops his hands and stares at me helplessly.

It doesn't take a mind reader to see Jack's putting it all together now. His hurt, roving gaze settles on me. It looks like he's out of it, the fugue or whatever it is, wherever he went.

"I guess so."

"You remember?"

"Yeah. I remember. I was furious."

"Do you have to get all Mr. Furious for it to happen?"

He takes the towel from me and walks back to the bathroom. I hear the water run once more, but this time he doesn't come back very quickly. Maybe he's staring into the mirror, thinking about things.

When Jack does return, I can tell he's been crying. His face is puffy and red, and his eyes look glazed. He sits down next to me and puts the towel on my face. God, that feels better.

"I don't know."

"Know what?"

"If I can do it without being angry." He holds his hands out in front of his chest and splays them out like a fan. "Shreve, I didn't even know I was doing it."

"I think you knew."

"Not really."

It's my turn to stay silent. His eyes are doing their thing, looking at other times, other places, remembering. He stays like that for a long while, and then he shuts his eyes tight against what he's seen.

"Yeah, I guess I knew." He shakes his head. "Yeah."

"Listen. We've gotta get out of here. Quincrux is gonna be coming for us. And the witch, Ilsa. You remember her now?"

"I think so. She wasn't . . . nice. She was inside me. She made me do what I didn't want to do." He shudders. I know how he feels. If I could wash my head out with Lava soap, I sure would have done it by now.

"Yeah. I don't know how you compartmentalize that."

"I . . . I didn't. I guess I knew if I was aware of it . . . I would've . . ."

I can feel the pressure building around him. He's about to go shockwave, and I don't think my head or face can take another blow. Who am I kidding? If he goes supernova now I'm dead.

"Jack! NO!"

He blinks. He clenches and unclenches his hands. He looks at me. Maybe it's something in my face, but the pressure eases.

"When I think of her . . . inside me . . . I don't think I can control it."

"You've got to. Jack. Man. This is important."

He nods, but his face is flushed and his eyes are narrow and his whole body has the aspect of the Angry Kid statue I saw earlier. Rigid and pissed the hell off. My ears pop again.

"Jack! I want you to stand up, go into the bathroom, and let loose there. Can you do that?"

A little muscle is popping in his cheek and cords are standing out on his neck, but he manages to nod again and stands stiffly. His walk to the shitter is slow and deliberate, like he's thinking about the placement of each footfall. I sit up, even though my head is killing me, and grab the mattress I'm lying on. I pull it off the bed and onto the floor, over my body.

I yell, "DO IT! DO IT, JACK! THINK OF WHAT THE WITCH DID TO—"

I hear a gigantic whoosh of air, an eruption of debris and paper ripping my posters and pictures and scattering my books across the floor, while the bunk beds make a horrible screeching wail and slide forward to slam into the wall. The sound is massive and painful. A fist of air slams into the mattress and shoves me along with it, and we go skidding off the floor and halfway out the front door. The desk chair is thrown so hard against the desk that one of the metal legs is bent at a jagged angle when it comes to rest.

Jesus H. He's volatile, my Jack.

I pull myself from underneath the mattress and see him standing in the doorway to the bathroom.

He gives me a bewildered look, and then he smiles sheepishly. "I think I broke the toilet. The metal bowl is kinda crumpled."

I laugh. "Holy smokes, man. You're like . . . I don't know . . . a superhero or something."

I stand, go to him, and stick out my hand, flat, palm up. Finally, he gets it and gives me some skin.

"I've got a plan, bro. And we're gonna have to do it quick. By tomorrow."

He nods, serious, and then he grins. "Hey, if I'm a superhero, does that make you my sidekick?"

I don't know if I'm more stunned by the fact Jack just made a joke or that it was at my expense.

"Don't get too big for your britches, man."

We laugh again, but it dies pretty quick because Booth stands in the doorway.

▪▪▪

"What the hell is going on here?"

It's official. I have, with Jack's help, unhinged Assistant Warden Horace Booth. His shirt is untucked, his hair, normally so neat and well groomed, is lopsided, and his expression is one of panicked bewilderment. I should feel better seeing him like this, but really it just scares me. Enemies are supposed to do their best, and he's not even trying.

"Answer me! I just put three boys in an ambulance bound for the hospital. Twenty boys have told me that you were present at the . . . altercation. And now this!"

He glares at the room. It looks like a tornado has come through the cell.

"Those boys were . . . Shreve, what happened to your face?"

Words are my thing. Words are my curse. But now, words are what might save us.

Jack looks at me expectantly.

"Ox. He wanted to do a fight club, made us challenge him. Hit me twice in the face. Then his face got all flushed, and he started spasming or something like he was having a seizure. Then he went crazy. I mean, buck-wild, throwing fists, knees, elbows, knocking desks everywhere.

"When Jack saw what was happening, he grabbed my arm, pulled me out the door. Ox caught Fishkill . . . I mean Jim . . . and Reasoner."

Jack looks at Booth, and—an uncaring god as my witness—he makes his eyes go all puppy-doggish. He looks at Booth like he's still terrified and nods emphatically. That kid, he keeps bringing the surprises.

Booth looks back and forth between the two of us. Then he slumps his shoulders and passes a hand over his face. The peacock is gone.

He walks to the desk—he's lucky it's bolted to the wall—uprights our single chair, and sits down heavily.

"Listen, boys. I'm trying to get my head around this. You're saying that Jeremy went crazy? Beat everyone up?"

I blink, look at Jack, and shrug. *Who's Jeremy?*

Booth sighs and throws his hands into the air. "Ox. Jeremy Williams."

I nod. "Yeah, that's what I'm saying."

"So what happened in here?" Booth looks at the disaster area that is our room.

I don't have any words for that. Jack and I remain silent.

Booth rubs his face again, like he hasn't had much sleep. Then he puts one hand on his knee in the Conan pose, elbow out.

"You see my problem? Something is going on around here. And I'm inclined to talk to the Warden, but I think she'd pack you all off to the Farm. Which might do you all some good." He waves a hand at me. "Or maybe not."

Booth pauses and squints, like he's trying to read my thoughts.

"For some reason, I can't shake the feeling that Mr. Quincrux . . . that he has something to do with all of this. I can't . . ."

I'm doing whatever I can to look nonchalant. I'd whistle if that wouldn't look incriminating. That name makes me want to run screaming from the room. God help us if Booth mentions the witch. Jack might explode.

"Ever since . . . ever since his interview with you boys . . . I've been having trouble . . ." He coughs. "Sleeping. Remembering things. And now it looks like Armageddon in here. What am I supposed to think?"

You'd hear crickets if this were a TV show. I don't know if I'd change the channel. I might stick around just to see what kind of trouble these kids get into.

Booth gives out a huge exhalation of air and stands, brushing his slacks. He looks down at himself, and I can see him going through a mental checklist. Shirt tucked? No? Now it is. Belt fastened and shiny? Check. Shoes sparkly? Check. Hair? He pats his head, and then he removes the black pick with the fist in the handle and swiftly addresses the situation.

We watch.

When he's done, he inhales, gets his chest looking right, puffed up and resembling a peacock. Then he puts his hands on his waist and glares at us. Booth is back.

"Come on, Shreve. Let's get you to the infirmary. Jack, you come too. I don't want to let you two out of my sight."

TEN

On the inside, you expand to fill your limitations. To find the limits of your world. Your place in it.

We're not precisely in prison. We do have freedom to wander the grounds. To use the bathroom in waking hours when we'd like. Wards may only enter their assigned wing, Commons, the cafeteria, the classrooms, the library. Admin is off-limits, unless summoned. Believe me, you don't want to be summoned to the Warden.

All three of us stand in the hallway outside the infirmary, one way leading back to Commons and the entrances to the various wings, and the other way leading to Admin and the exit. All Mrs. Cheeves, the nurse, did was slap an Insta-Freeze cold pack on my face and pump me full of ibuprofen.

Booth glares at us. "As you're so happy to point out often, Shreve, I'm just the Assistant Warden, which means the next eight hours of my time will be spent filling out forms in triplicate and reviewing all the video of the classroom and classroom hallway."

"There's a camera in the classroom?" I glance at Jack.

Booth smiles a cat-about-to-pounce-smile. "Why, yes, there is. Didn't you know that?"

I might have paled. Just a little, though, and only for a moment. "Wait a sec. So there's cameras in the classrooms? How come you never used them to bust me?"

It's Booth's turn to pale. He opens his mouth, and then he shuts it.

I pat his arm. "Hey, it's okay. I'm out of the business anyway, Assistant Warden."

His face purples until it resembles . . . well, half of mine. For a second he looks like he wants to rip me apart with his bare hands.

But then he throws back his shoulders and laughs.

He laughs.

He grabs me and pulls me into him, to his chest, in a big bear hug. I don't quite know what to do. It's inappropriate physical contact, of course, and I might be able to make some kind of trouble for him about it. But I can smell the man. Part cologne, part hair product, a taint of sweat and . . . well . . . him.

For a moment I think of the words *parens patriae* engraved over the entrance to the commons. Part of me wants to punch, scratch, kick—*anything*—not to have this contact. This closeness, never looked for. Never asked for.

But that moment's gone, and he has me in his grip.

He's not trying very hard to be the best enemy he can be right now. But there's no indication he's going to let me go anytime soon. So I hug back. What else am I supposed to do? He's not that bad a guy.

When he's done, he holds me out at arm's length, tears streaming from his eyes, and peers at me.

"Shreve, be careful, will you? I don't know what's going on around here, but I know you." He releases my arms. "I know you. And you're as reckless as the day is long. I don't want to see you get hurt." Booth laughs again and wipes the tears from his face and points at my mug. "Any more hurt."

My smile makes it feel like the flesh of my cheek is being drawn tight across a drum. I'm trying not to do it, trying not to smile back at him, because it hurts and because that's not what we do at each other. He's supposed to be my nemesis, for crying out loud. I don't have a center point anymore if I don't have Booth to fight against.

"Get yourselves back to your room. For today, I don't want you roaming around until I get a handle on what's going on."

I nod. But I have no intention of doing what he says. That feels good, to get to disobey him again. Seems like old times.

Booth jangles off toward Admin, and I wait until he's out of sight. Then I say to Jack, "If you tell anyone about that, I'll kill you." We've got to run. Now. But we've got to get back to the cell first. "C'mon," I tell Jack. "We'll get all my money, which isn't too much, but enough. And we'll get my secret weapons."

ELEVEN

On the inside, change always comes with some pain. My face throbs as we walk down the hall back to Commons. The double doors in front of us swing open, and there's Sloe-Eyed Norman pushing his way through. He looks at us with his soft eyes and opens his mouth as if to say something.

A little shiver of alarm runs down my spine, and I put a hand on Jack's arm to stop him.

When the door swings all the way open, he stands there, behind Norman, dressed somberly and neat.

Quincrux.

And beside him, licking her lips, the witch.

"Run!" I wheel, not before catching surprised expressions from the trio, and dash back down the hall.

Suddenly, I feel him. Him. Trying to get in.

I stop. I can't help myself. He's in. I turn around to look.

There's Quincrux looking at me, boring into me. I try and conjure the jawbreaker in my mind's eye, but he's too powerful. I can feel his laughter inside my head, his scorn at my defenses.

But I'm still incarcerado, still in my flesh enough to see that Jack has become the Angry Kid statue. Mr. Furious. Jack Sprat, about to jump the candle.

"Jack!" It's all I can do to scream his name. That's the last bit of me I can muster under the assault from Quincrux. He's a machine, a monster, Godzilla trampling Tokyo. And then—I don't know if it's Quincrux violating my mind, or if it's my mind—I feel an intense need to possess something, to consume something. And I fight, I squirm and writhe using that part of me that is nothing but me—that infinitesimal spark that's not blood, not bone, not flesh, but solely Shreve. Like a tadpole in a palm, I fight, I squirm. Like a cricket caught in gigantic hands, I twist and turn and move to find my way out. Finally I feel one path with less resistance, and I follow it. I see a quick image of myself, clad in orange, stopped midstride in a hallway, looking backward over my shoulder with a curious expression of terror and fierceness and stubbornness. And I realize I'm looking out of his eyes. I'm feeling his feelings and thinking his thoughts. And that terrifies me. Because, on the inside, he's not as loathsome as I would have thought. He's far, far worse.

But then his assault stops and I'm whisked away, out of his mind. I'm back incarcerado in my own body, watching the air dimple.

The witch has her hands balled at her sides. I think she's smiling but I can't be sure, because the air is wavering and now my ears have popped.

"Jack! The witch!" I turn and run. "Remember what she did! She raped you!"

Jack goes supernova.

The shockwave picks me up, and I'm an orange pinwheel with no greater purpose than trying to minimize the damage when I hit the floor.

Tuck the chin, the teachers used to tell us in PE. Tuck the chin and pull the knees in tight.

I hit the tiles rolling and experience the intense sensation of my flesh moving separately from my skeleton. My muscles, my fat, all my soft tissue bounces back against the brutal impact of my knees cracking on the floor, my elbows and hands smashing into the green tiles. I feel like a thawed frozen turkey tossed from a window, rubbery and without volition.

I push myself up on hands skinned raw and stand.

Holy smokes.

Jack's standing over three people, panting.

I race down the hall toward him.

Sure enough, there's Quincrux, the witch, and poor Norman.

They've been blown back through the doors and into Commons, and fifty or sixty faces of boys look at us. Quincrux lies half on top of Ilsa, and Norman is underneath a table. I run to him. My elbows and knees are sore, my hands bleeding and raw, but I go down and crawl underneath a Commons table. Norman's there, amid a scattering of dominoes, with blood pouring out his mouth and nose.

"Oh no. Oh no."

Quincrux's leg is twisted at a horrible angle away from his body. His dark suit looks wet, and something pokes at the fabric of the pants. I'm betting a bone.

Ilsa.

Her neck is twisted horribly. If she's not dead now, she will be soon.

Jack stands in the hallway, looking dazed. His hands hang limp at his sides. I push up, back on my feet. The boys in the general pop stare at me like I've sprouted fur and fangs. They step back.

"We've got to run. Quincrux will wake soon. And he'll control us."

Jack doesn't respond.

"Jack! We've got to run!" I grab his arm and drag him behind me. He's sluggish. He can't be thinking good thoughts right now. Too much blood. Behind us, fire alarms sound.

By the time we're passing the infirmary, Mrs. Cheeves steps into the hallway, surprised to find two wards barreling down the hallway.

"They're hurt! Call an ambulance." I don't pause to see how she reacts.

Finally Jack's feet move of his own accord.

I take a second to glance at him as we bolt down the hall, and he looks lost and hurt. Tears stream from his eyes, and his hand feels dead in mine as I pull him along.

We reach Admin. The bulls and administrators, men and women, are rushing toward us, so I point back down the hall. "There's been an explosion!" I yell. Some of them pass us, running toward Commons.

Booth appears from an office, popping up over cubicle walls like a well-groomed prairie dog.

"Are you okay? Shreve? Jack?" He grabs my shoulder and turns me toward him. "Are you injured?" God, there's real concern for us on his face.

"No. But something happened back there. They need you."

Another alarm goes off, and Booth turns from us toward Commons.

"You two stay here."

And then we're standing in Admin, with just one guard between us and freedom. He's at the front doors, manning the metal detectors. Right now he's half-standing from his seat and looking right at us.

"Jack, you're gonna have to do it again."

His face crumples.

"No. I can't. I . . ." The waterworks really flow now, and as I notice it on him, I realize I'm flowing pretty good, too. Norman was a good guy. A real good guy. He didn't deserve that.

"We have to. We have to. So no one else gets hurt."

"No, I won't."

"It was the witch. The witch was there. And Quincrux. They would've ridden us. They would've raped us from the inside out."

"She might be dead."

"Yeah. But it wasn't your fault." I don't know what to do. I take Jack by the shoulders and shake him like trailer trash shaking an infant. "It wasn't your fault!"

He gives me a look, a look like he's buried under an avalanche and will take all winter to dig himself out. He's going away, retreating into his safe place, and I can't really blame him.

I give it the last gasp. "We don't have much time. What if she wakes up? She'll invade all of them, and they'll come after us. And then—"

"I don't care."

He's broken. He slumps to the floor.

It doesn't take a mind reader to know Jack's out of play. I'd say borderline catatonic. Definitely in shock.

I'm going to have to do this by myself.

■ ■ ■

I don't know this guard's name. He's not an inside bull. He's an Admin bull, which means he's not used to seeing us wards in orange. He doesn't know how to deal with the likes of me.

I need to believe that. He doesn't know how to deal with the likes of me.

I trot over to him, and he stands up straight.

"Please stay behind the yellow line, son."

He's long and gawky with a face full of pimples. He reminds me a little of Barney Fife, but without the geniality.

I step over the line. That's what I do. A line-stepper, I am.

"Behind the line, son."

"You're like three years older than me."

Huh. That's not the best way to start this exchange.

"Behind the line." He puts his hand on his belt. His fingers come to rest on his Taser.

God, this is taking too long. They're going to be coming for us—if not Quincrux, then Booth and the rest of the Admin-dwellers.

"Booth needs your help. There's been an explosion."

"Fat chance." The bull snorts and draws the Taser from its holster. "He didn't say anything to me. I think I'll stick here."

I feel pressure building, and this time it's not coming from Jack. I'm starting to understand how Jack feels, because the anger I usually tamp down or deflect with wisecracking or insults is starting to shift inside me. It's anger at a universe that has dealt me a crappy hand all around. I think of my drunk of a mother. Of her neglect of me. Of Vig. I think of the way tectonic plates shift and rub each other over millennia, or glaciers wear away bedrock. There are things, vast things, moving inside me after years of quiet.

If Quincrux and the witch can do it, why can't I?

I look him in the eyes. His name is Marvin Robinson.

I wish I took that from his mind. But it doesn't take a mind reader to read the name tag on his uniform.

I try and remember what it felt like to have Quincrux battering at my gates. How did it feel to have him rape me? Rape. That's what it was. Maybe not physically, but he took something without asking. He invaded. He left me open and abused and violated. How did it feel?

Disconnected, and more connected than anything I can even bear.

I think about Quincrux. I know him. I've been inside him, too, the same way he's been inside me. I've looked through his eyes.

"You have to go help. People are hurt."

"Step behind the line, or I'll be forced to tase you."

Marvin Robinson brings up the Taser, and I look at him. And remembering how it felt, I send out the part of me that is me but not me. I send out the detachable part of Shreveport Justice Cannon, the part that isn't locked incarcerado, the part that can fly, that can lift itself out of the meatsuit like I was dancing the Ghost Dance. That part, I send out.

A lot is going on inside Marvin Robinson's head. But one thing is clear: he's pretty excited at the prospect of tasing me.

It's a weird little dance my soul does then. I'm in Marvin Robinson's head when he pulls the Taser trigger—*That rotten kid, he deserves it!*—but I'm also back incarcerado in my own body. My perception of time thickens like molasses. The Taser darts lance slowly through the air. I move like a fly caught in syrup as the blue electric sparks cross the yellow line. Marvin Robinson didn't really want me to stay behind the line. The darts are slowing, slowing, slowing as they near, and I can't move fast enough out to get of the way.

The darts bite into my chest, and suddenly the whole world goes bright white. For a horrible instant of jittering and contortion, my skeleton becomes neon and flickers on and off at some frequency beyond the physical body's understanding other than AAAIIIEEEE. And then . . . I squirm. I squirm like that good old tadpole in a child's hand. But it's more than my body squirming—it's me, all of me that matters. And I slip out and race back up the Taser line, up the fuse, through and past the dart, through the Taser, and into Marvin. And I kick his ass out.

The bastard. I'm in charge now.

The me/not me equilibrium stabilizes. MeMarvin yanks the Taser wire and darts out of the MeIncarcerado body.

Time is running out.

MeIncarcerado walks forward and kicks MeMarvin square in the nuts.

I feel it on both ends, the kick and the pain. It hurts like someone has jabbed a burning pike deep into MeMarvin's guts, and I don't like that. That part of my awareness skitters and cringes away from the blow, out and away from Marvin. Discorporeal. Then I blink and I'm just me again, and Marvin the guard kneels before me.

I kick him in the face. Something goes crunchy there.

He probably won't look much like Barney Fife anymore.

He doesn't get up.

I take his keys. I take his Taser. I take his wallet.

In the end, everything he has, I've taken it from him.

If I'm as evil as Quincrux and the witch, then so be it. The difference between them and me is that I don't have a choice.

There's not much time.

I run back to Jack. He's looking at me, wide-eyed and surprised. It doesn't take a mind reader to know he's picked up on my little trick.

I jerk him up off the floor, and we run out the front doors of Casimir Pulaski Juvenile Detention Center and into the parking lot. I'm pushing the beeper button on Marvin's keychain like a madman and waiting to hear the chirp of the car alarm system. It's hard to hear over the whine of the sirens coming from inside Casimir. But finally it comes.

Beep.

The doors are unlocked now. Jack's not crying anymore as I push him into the car and slide behind the wheel.

We're free.

TWELVE

On the inside, nothing ever changes. So everything outside appears strange and new now.

I drive through the trailer park, just to make sure it isn't swarming with police. It looks different. The trailers look shabbier, more run-down. They're dented and desperate, perched on the edge of town by the big piney woods.

We sit in the car on a gravel access road behind a cheap cinder-block strip mall. We're a few miles down from the trailer park. We'll hoof it from here.

Jack rummages through the car and finds a gym bag with shorts, sweatpants, and a couple T-shirts. It all smells like dog balls and mildew.

We change in the car. There's just enough clothing to keep us safe from indecency charges if they retake us.

Having seen the inside of Marvin's sadistic noggin, I halfway expected Jack to find a gun while searching the car. Part of me really hoped he would. If I'm to be a fugitive, then I'd like to be an armed fugitive at least. But I still have the Taser and its holster. The holster sports a couple of blocky cartridges. I might be able to figure out how to reload the thing.

We're parked in a brake of hardwoods, still within earshot of the interstate. The constant hiss of cars is comforting and threatening all at once. The road is freedom, but the road will bring the law, too. Damn, I'm starting to sound like a country song.

We wait for dark.

▪▪▪

"What was your secret weapon?" Jack asks. He's sitting in the passenger seat, looking out the front windshield at the cottonwoods shedding their fluff like snow. His feet are on the dash, and if I squint it looks like he's in a fetal position. But at least he's come out of his daze. I can tell he's pretty torn up about hurting them. Killing them, maybe.

We're born into pain, and we leave in pain, and we cause it along the way too, it seems. It's a damned hard lesson.

And how do I feel about it? I'm just as guilty, I guess. But Quincrux and the witch had it coming to them, the rapists.

Norman was a sweetheart. God, I hope he's okay.

I look at Jack. Really look at him. He repeats his question. "Come on. What was your secret weapon?"

"Trash bags."

He laughs. "You gotta tell me how."

"You know. Road crews of convicts. We bust out, run for it. The minute we're safe, we start picking up trash. Nobody would question us then, even with the orange jumpers. We'd just be another detail cleaning up the city's mess."

Jack smiles. "Not bad. It wouldn't have worked. But not bad." He pauses and then says, "Do you remember when they took us over?"

"Yeah."

"You remember what they were talking about? How Quincrux couldn't get . . . get inside me? Cause he'd been weakened."

"Yeah. And he said the witch was there because of her talent with 'supernumeraries.'"

"But he warned her not to go somewhere. 'The incident in Maryland.' He said he was recovering. It's something to think about."

"What? You mean go there?"

"We go there, they wouldn't follow."

"But whatever happened to them could happen to us." It's weird being the voice of reason. Normally I rely on other people to talk me out of stuff. "Quincrux and the witch are . . ."

I pause on that particular be verb. It could be "was," depending on how bad the witch's neck was twisted. But I won't shed a single damned tear over her sorry demise. If that makes me evil, so be it.

I keep going. "They're adults and more powerful than—"

"Us?"

"Yeah."

"How did you do it?"

"Do what?"

"Don't lie to me, Shreve. I just want to know." Jack holds up his hand and shows it to me. Making a point, he is. I remember a similar conversation, not a week ago, but with me asking the questions.

I put up my hand, near his. There's eleven fingers, right there.

"You mean, how did I take out the guard?"

"Yeah. That. You did the same trick Quincrux and the witch did."

I think for a bit. I can't come up with an answer for him.

"I don't know, Jack. Maybe something transferred into me when Quincrux . . ." I don't know any other way to say it, and it hurts to admit it, even to Jack. "When he raped me. I think part of him, his residue or something, was left behind."

Jack leans back in the seat. It's a shabby little car. The seats are fabric that's gone nappy, and the whole inside has the scent of a washed ashtray. I doubt the great state of Arkansas pays Marvin too well.

"So, you can do what they do?"

"I don't know." This kid is getting me worried, acting like this is a problem. And I don't even know what this is. "No. I don't know. It just happened. I thought, 'If they can do it, why can't I?'"

Jack bows his head. His face darkens, looking grim.

Finally, he looks up and stares at me with hard, gray eyes.

"Good. This is good." The way he says it doesn't sound like it's good. Jack shifts in his seat and looks back toward the falling cottonwood dander. "I need you to promise me something."

I don't like making promises, honestly. I never have. I never will. But this is Jack.

"I . . . I can try, man. What is it?"

"It's simple. Promise me you'll never do to someone else what Quincrux and Ilsa did to us."

It's my turn to bow my head now. I put my hand on the door handle.

"No." I tense, alert for any sign of Jack going explodey. "No, I can't. I can't tell you I'll never do it. If I have to protect us, I will. If I have to do it to stop them, I'll do it. All I can promise is that I'll try to never do it to someone who doesn't deserve it,"

Jack looks at me—that long, faraway gaze seeing other places, other people—and for a moment I think he's going to start his magic shoving match. But then he shakes away his thoughts and nods once in acknowledgment.

I blow air. I didn't realize I was quite so tense. I pull out the Taser and holster and try to remove the cartridge from the barrel. My chest burns and aches where the needles pierced my skin and delivered the charge. But the Taser has a good feel in my hand.

After a few moments of fiddling with the thing, I pop off the cartridge, shift it to my other hand, and pull another cartridge from the holster. The cartridges hold the needles and wires that zapped the pee-waddly-doo out of me. Nice heft. There's one more left in the holster. On back of the Taser, a glowing blue battery charge icon reads half-full. I don't know whether that means I have one shot left or means Marvin tased unruly wards before me, draining the charge.

It's heavier than I thought a Taser would be. But it is comforting.

We wait for dark.

▪▪▪

We trudge away from Little Rock, from the glowing indigent spillage of strip-malls and convenience stores into the green. We hike through the piney woods with the moon rising, pale but bright, illuminating the mat of pine needles. There's a trail that loops through an old hobo camp that in the summer becomes a small tent city. Now, with fall coming on, it's bare. Trash flutters in the wind, and a charcoal pit remains, naked and angry, like God extinguished his Kool amid the evergreens and hardwoods.

"We used to play all through these woods. They stretch about six or seven miles until you hit the railyard. There's a little pond over that way." I point off into the trees. "We've got lots of forts scattered about."

"Forts?"

"Eh. Really just holes with brush and plywood scraps. For Kick the Can and Army. Capture the Flag."

The look Jack gives me makes me stop. He's never heard of these games.

"You mean you've never played Capture the Flag?"

"No . . . I . . ." He gets this panicked look, like if he

answers the question wrong something terrible will happen. This kid isn't like any kid I've ever met. He's never had a day of fun in his life.

I've got to change that. For his sake. For my sake. Believe it or not, I've had fun growing up, even with the Moms as she is. Me and Vig and Coco and even some of the Garcia boys from down the way... we've had good times here in these woods.

"Hey, it's cool. We'll play it someday. Soon. You'll love it."

Jack's smile looks more like a grimace.

"What's gonna happen when we get to your house?" he asks.

"I'm gonna grab my stash—I've got a little money—and get us some clothes. Some real clothes. Food. I've got to find out how Vig's doing..."

Jack nods, leaving me to my thoughts.

Vig's gonna be a problem. Jack and I can't stay with Moms. Maybe long enough for a shower, packing the bags, digging up my stash. But after that we've got to roll. There's no safety here.

We come through the piney woods and into the gully that separates the trailer park from the trees. A single bright halogen bulb is mounted on a pole in the middle of a handful of building blocks. The trailers look crumpled and beaten in its white light. I can hear the sounds of dinner being cleared away, the slamming of screen doors through paper-thin walls. Radios and televisions blare into the autumn night.

Coco's trailer is lit up like a carnival, Halloween decorations glowing in every window. Her room light is on. I was supposed to write her. I meant to write. But it was all so hard. And what was I going to say? Hey, girl, you know how your dad didn't like me? Well he's gonna love me now!

We creep up the gully embankment, up onto the shabby, eroding plateau that holds the Holly Pines Trailer Park.

"Gotta wait here for a bit. There are folks about. It takes a while for the park to settle down."

Looks like Billy Cather's got himself a new truck, the bastard. I must have totaled the old one. That makes me happy. He did keep a gun in his cab, I remember. Something to think about.

"That trailer there." I point. "He shot me. Right here, through the arm."

"For real?"

"For real."

"What did you do?"

"Whatdya mean, 'What did I do?'" I put on my best expression of innocence. "I didn't do nothing."

"Right. You don't get shot for doing nothing."

"I stole his truck."

Jack laughs. It's a silent laugh, with his head down and his mouth open, like it's the funniest thing he's ever heard in his life—so funny he can't even make a sound. I believe the little bastard is laughing at me.

"Hey. It wasn't that funny."

When Jack's done laughing, tears are streaming away from the corners of his eyes.

"Hey, man." I guess I'm a little hurt he finds my pain so damn funny. "Uncool."

"Why? Why would you do something like that?"

What can I say? The longer Jack is with me, the clearer it will become to him that I'm an idiot.

"Went stir-crazy and tried to bolt."

"Stir-crazy?"

"Man, you think Casimir is the only prison?"

"No." He shifts, uncomfortable on the clay and slate embankment. "I guess not."

Sighing, I say, "I wish I hadn't. I've done a lot of stupid things but—"

"You think Quincrux will come here?"

That's a change of gears.

"Definitely."

Jack does something I've never heard him do before. He curses. "Then I can't be seen here."

"Why not?"

"As far we know, the only person they want is me. They don't know anything about your . . ." He stops, not knowing what to call it. "Power."

"Yet. Quincrux will pull it from Marvin if he interviews him."

"Oh."

"And don't forget the witch. She's put me on her

grocery list."

We're silent for a while, and then I say, "There's nothing for it except to get in and get out as fast as possible."

"Let's do it, then. You think it's late enough?"

The sky's fully dark, and the stars shine hard and brilliant above. There's still some movement and noise in the park, but that might be better.

"Yeah. Here we go."

I leave the Taser on the ground, marking its position. No need to have an armed homecoming.

We scramble up the rest of the embankment and across the alley behind the row of trailers. It's just a gravel path where most families keep their trashcans and assorted junk: used toys, broken bicycles, moldering plywood, broken TV sets, collapsed lawn chairs, rakes and shovels, portable deer blinds, tires. There's a reason why folks call us trailer trash.

Up and across the alley we run. Moms's trailer is right here. The tin awning is slumping to the right of the door now, but other than that, the trailer looks the way it was six months ago when I ended up upside-down, bleeding out in Billy Cather's truck.

Moms's Delta 88 is parked behind us. Busted headlight and crumpled fender. That's new.

I reach for the doorknob, then stop. What's going to happen here? I can feel a hard ball of tension in my gut. My hand shakes, and Jack notices it.

Moms has two speeds: raging bitch and oblivious

drunk. Which one will we get?

I'm just about to turn around and run back to the woods—this can wait till later—when Jack puts his hand on my arm and squeezes. It's just a little thing, but it helps.

I turn the handle, push open the door, and step inside.

"Moms! I'm home!"

She's standing in the kitchenette, holding a big knife, her eyes wide.

"Shree. Holy Christ. You nearly scared me to death." She stops, tosses the knife on the linoleum counter, and cocks her head at Jack. "With company, looks like."

The house stinks of smoke. Overfull ashtrays and fast-food wrappers are everywhere. Judging by the number of cans lying around, one of Moms's friends is partial to Milwaukee's Best Light.

She's dressed in a waitress outfit, blue with white edges and a nametag that reads Margaret. She must have wheedled her way back in at the Waffle House since the last time she was fired. At least she's not tricking. Her face is drawn, and her blue eyes are rheumy and glazed. When I was a kid she'd pull out old high school yearbooks and show us pictures of herself and Dad, holding hands, in funny outfits and bad haircuts. She looked beautiful in those pictures. Now her drunk's belly and her spider arms give her a gnomish look. She's wrinkled and ugly and a ghost of that person in the yearbooks. That person is gone, like water boiling away in a pan and just leaving the crusty hard minerals baked into the sides.

"I see you've done some decorating, Moms."

"What happened to your face?"

"Had a little accident on the way home."

No answer. She opens a cabinet and pulls out a full bottle of Heavenly Hill vodka. She cracks the seal. It takes her a second to find a semi-clean cup in the pile of dishes rising from the sink.

"But thanks for your concern," I say, letting it cut through.

Still nothing.

She pours for four or five seconds, puts down the booze, and turns and pulls a two-liter NuGrape from the mini-fridge. Our old fridge is dead and sitting behind the trailer in the alley, just waiting for some kid to climb in and pull the door shut. She pours enough in the cup to change the color of the vodka, but that's about it.

She chugs her cup. Bam. Knocking it back.

She mixes another, moves to the kitchenette table, pushes some cans aside, and sits down.

I'm trying to peep her, to get inside. But I can't seem to get to the place inside me where I can make the Ghost Dance work. Maybe it's the knot in my stomach. Maybe it's the hole in my heart. I'm incarcerado in my own body. I've only done it once before. Just once to Marvin. I've only got ten fingers. Maybe it was a fluke. Maybe I'm just a run-of-the-mill, everyday, average kid with a drunk mother.

"Yeah, and thanks for all the stuff too."

She pulls a pack of cigarettes from her outfit's apron

pocket, taps out a smoke, and tamps the loose tobacco by hitting it on the tabletop. I've seen her do that a thousand times if I've seen her do it once.

"What stuff?" She says it, but I can tell she's not even interested. It doesn't take a mind reader to know I'm not high on her list of priorities.

"All the stuff you brought me when you visited."

Her eyes go Grinchy, and she smiles.

"The mouth on you. No change there." She takes a big slurp of the NuGrape and V.

"The mouth on you. That hasn't changed much either." That's about as close as I've ever come to calling her a drunk.

"How'd you get out? They told me you'd be in for eighteen months."

I've got to be careful here.

"Sorry to break up the party. It looks like it was a good one."

"Shree, the little preacher. Spare me the sermon."

"Where's Vig?"

"Not here."

I'm terrified of what I might see inside Vig when he gets home, of whether he'll be broken, crusty, and resentful, used up. Whether he'll be a husk of the kid he could have been.

"Whose trailer is he staying in? Why didn't you get him after work?"

She stands up, goes back to the vodka, and makes another drink. Then she opens a cabinet and pulls out an envelope. She tosses the paper at me.

I snatch it.

"He's not here," she repeats.

The letter is from Social Services, dated not long after my arrest. Vig's been removed from the "unfit living conditions" and placed in a foster home, by order of Judge David Vernor. If Vig's legal guardian, Margaret Cannon, can prove to the state's satisfaction that the living conditions at the "residence of origin" have improved, can show proof of employment and a certificate of inspection by health services, then the court will consider "placing" Vigor back in the "residence of origin" after an additional assessment period of six months.

There's the address of the foster home. There's a phone number. I stuff the paper into my pocket.

He's gone.

Moms is looking into her cup as she's always done. She's not looking at me.

I'm so furious that my body feels filled with too much blood. My face feels so swollen it might pop, spraying blood everywhere.

Vig. My little dude is gone, and all I have is this piece of worn, alcohol-soaked leather.

"Do you even feel ashamed?"

"Ashamed? Of course I do. I'm ashamed of you. You brought this on us."

My heart's hammering in my chest, and my hands are shaking more. I want to strangle her.

"*I* brought?"

"You've always been a selfish little brat, aintcha, Shree?" She wipes her mouth, then raises the cigarette and takes a long drag from it and expels the blue smoke at my face. "You never thought of anyone but yourself, did ya? Didn't think about anyone else when you were stealing that truck. Didn't think about anyone else, you crappy kid."

"I'm not the goddamned mother here—"

She stands bolt upright. "Don't you take the Lord's name! Don't you take it!"

God, I hate her. She doesn't care about the Lord or Jesus or anyone else. It's just theatrics. Just a stick to beat me with. A rule she can cite.

I try again to get in her head. I've got the fuel of fifteen years of neglect like napalm at my back, and I try to get in.

Slipping behind her eyes is so easy it's like sticking a branch in a pool and making no ripples.

A cesspool.

The things she's done. The thing's she's had done to her. Family can support you. Family can ruin you forever.

There are things that happen in this world, and we'll never get out from under the weight of them. Never. It'll take a bottle or a gun to stop the suffering.

MeIncarcerado thrums with inaction, my muscles tight and rigid, the bruised side of my face pounding like a war drum. I fly through her internal cellblocks, through her long dark hallways, looking inside each one with door upon barred door. None of them pretty, none of them holding sweet memories. Where I can, I close them—close off the images to my sight, and maybe to hers.

It's just a moment. And then it's over.

Jack says, "Shreve, you're bleeding."

I wipe my nose. There's blood on the back of my hand.

Moms is standing there poleaxed, holding her cup loosely in one hand, her cigarette in the other, staring at me but not staring at the same time. She sets down the cup and snubs out her smoke.

I take two steps, and I've got her in the circle of my arms, squeezing her. I don't think I've ever hugged her before, and I don't know what's making me do it now. Maybe it's because when Booth hugged me, that felt good. And I knew, for a moment at least, that someone gave a damn about me.

Moms fights it hard, pulling her arms up and pushing me away. She shoves at my shoulders, but the vodka has already taken effect. She's sloppy and weak, but still mean as a snake.

"Get off of me, you little bastard." She bats at my head, and one of her hands clips my cheek. My face explodes with pain, a white light behind my eyes. But I hold on to her. I hold on to her as tight as I can, because I'll probably never get another chance. This is my mom. This is her, and I still hate her for what she's done to me and Vig, but I can see what made her how she is and can start to forgive her. Maybe. Just a little.

After a while she stops struggling and lets her arms drop.

When I let her go, she slumps back into the kitchenette chair.

She holds up her chipped coffee cup and says, "Make me a good one, Shree, honey. Okay? You always make them good."

She likes them strong.

I take the cup and go to the mini-fridge. It looks like she's been living off burritos from the Quik-Mart and whatever they give her at the Waffle House. I pour her three fingers of Heavenly Hill and a shot of NuGrape. I sprinkle a little salt in, just a touch. That's my secret. She likes them salty.

I give her the cup. She drinks.

"Oh, that's good, Shree."

"Moms?"

"Yeah, Shree? Can you find something on the TV for me?"

She moves to the couch. I follow. Jack looks at me with a curious and pained expression, one I can't read.

We go through the ritual established so long ago: me the dutiful son, her the lounging queen. I clean off the table at her right elbow while she leans into the armrest of the couch and sips her drink, feet tucked underneath her, staring into the flickering light of the television. I take the ashtray, so full it's hard to pick up without spilling butts, and bring it to the kitchenette trash bin, also full. Somehow I get all the butts into the trash. I wipe out the ashtray with a Taco Bell wrapper and return it to her side table.

Jack looks at me, raises his eyebrows.

My face is throbbing and flushed as I take off her shoes and get her feet up on the small ottoman.

If there's a clean place in the whole trailer, it's around the TV.

"Moms?"

"Honey, why do you have to call me that?"

"What?"

"Moms. You used to call me momma."

"It's just one of those things, Moms."

"I don't like it. It's like you're saying I'm . . . I don't know . . ."

"More than one."

"Yeah, like that. Like I'm more than one person."

We're all more than one person. But I don't say that.

"Okay, momma. Okay."

She lights another cigarette and sips her drink.

I go to the TV and flip through the channels.

"You want *Dancing*, *CSI*, or this movie?"

She thinks for a little while. "*Dancing*, hon. They dance so good. And they're not even real dancers."

I change the channels for her.

"Okay. Momma?"

"Yeah, hon?"

"It's good to see you."

"Did you see that twirl? She used to have her own TV show, but now she's dancing. It's dadblamed amazing how talented they are."

"Jack and I are going back to my room. Is my stuff still there?"

She doesn't answer. We leave her to it.

▪▪▪

In my room, I grab an old school backpack and my army duffle bag. The dresser is still stuffed with our clothing, mine and Vig's. I pick up his dinosaur T-shirt. I lift it up to my nose. It doesn't smell like him anymore, just stale cigarette smoke.

Under the mattress I find my stash, still there, in a cigar box. Seventy-three dollars and change. Mostly taken from cars in Holly Pines. It's wrong, but you do what you have to do.

We change clothes. My jeans are too big for Jack, and we have to find a belt and roll the legs. I grab a couple extra pair of shoes and shove them in the duffle. In my closet, I rummage around and get my survival kit—another cigar box, this one with matches, a pocketknife, some twine, some nylon rope, and a compass.

When we're packed, I sit down on my bed and Jack comes over to me, sits down, and doesn't say anything as I cry.

Huge sobs rip out of me, hurling out there for Jack to see. It's like a cough I can't control, with bits of my lungs coming up and out. Messy and raw. I feel like a boat rolling over in the sea, hull exposed. I feel like a car-struck dog, too injured to crawl under the porch.

I cry. Jack watches.

When I finally stop, he puts his hand on my shoulder and gives a long squeeze.

That's all.

"I'm so sorry, Shreve." Jack's said this before, but it's always been about something he's done.

I wipe my nose. It's not bleeding anymore, but it is running like a faucet. My throat is sore.

"Don't be."

"I can't even begin to—"

"Then don't."

I'm everything she said I am. Selfish. Here I am crying about what a rough deal I've got, what a crappy mother I have. And Jack, the orphan, the homeless kid, the parent-killer, he tells me he's sorry. I'm a fool.

Moms continues to stare into the TV as we come out. I make her a last drink before we leave. Then we walk out through the park and into the woods.

PART TWO:
WILD BLUE YONDER

Our two souls therefore, which are one,

Though I must go, endure not yet

A breach, but an expansion,

Like gold to airy thinness beat.

—John Donne, “A Valediction: Forbidding Mourning”

Well, as a spaniel is to water, so is a man to his own self. I will not give in because I oppose it—I do!—not my pride, not my spleen, nor any other of my appetites, but I do—I! Is there no single sinew in the midst of this that serves no appetite of Norfolk's but is, just, Norfolk? There is! Give that some exercise, my lord!

—Thomas More, in *A Man for All Seasons* by Robert Bolt

Off we go into the wild blue yonder,

Climbing high into the sun;

Here they come zooming to meet our thunder,

At 'em boys, Give 'er the gun! (Give 'er the gun!)

—"The Air Force Song" by Robert MacArthur Crawford

THIRTEEN

In the end, Jack relents. I spend less and less time incarcerado and more time out in the wide blue yonder.

I'm fifteen. I can't get a job. I don't have a driver's license. And I've got a record. Jack is just thirteen. Two kids alone in the wilderness, two kids alone in the city, they can't make it by themselves. Not without some manipulation. Not without some help.

I've learned what my destiny is, out here.

I'm a judge.

You can't lie to me.

▪▪▪

We spent a week in the piney woods west of the Holly Pines Trailer Park before a train came through. We'd turned near feral, living off pasta, jerky, chips, flat soda, and anything else we could buy at the interstate turnpike Git-N-Go. Seventy-three dollars doesn't go very far these days, it seems.

During the day, perched between the rails and the dark green of the piney woods, we watched for trains. It's not quite the Old West around here. Not a lot of rail traffic. At night we crept back to the safety of the woods.

Occasionally we'd hear the buzz of ATVs and motorcycles burning through the forest. But they never came too near. The weather turned colder, and we made wood fires to stay warm and slept in beds of pine needles.

▪▪▪

"Jack, how much do you remember of going all explodey?"

"Don't call it that."

"Well, what should I call it?"

"I don't know. But saying 'explodey' makes it sound like a trick or something."

"Well, it is kinda a trick, isn't it?"

He shook his head. "I don't know how to tell you."

"Try." I raised my hands, heading off the hurt looks. "I just want to understand."

"It comes from pain."

Silence.

There's not much I could say to that. Not much more than we're born into pain, and we leave in it, too. It's our constant companion. I hate it, but it's true and I've never seen otherwise.

"And I put up with it. So, so long. As long as I can. But the anger builds, and I want to shove it away from me."

"So, it's like a super-shove? Like you're just shoving everything away from you?"

"When it hurts bad enough."

▪▪▪

Sometimes I would take out the paper with Vig's foster home address and stare at it, dreaming of ways to get to him.

Sometimes, with Jack in tow, I'd creep to the gully and watch Coco's trailer. Jack stayed silent—maybe from hunger, maybe from sympathy. We didn't talk much.

But how could I contact Coco or Vig? Quincrux could show up at any time. He'd be sure to possess them, strip-mine their memories, and know that we were nearby.

So we waited for trains, and I thought about Coco and Vig, and we lived in the woods. A miserable existence.

It was maybe six or seven days since the breakout, and Jack was lying on the tracks, his ear to the rail.

"It's coming."

"What?"

"The train."

And it did. When it neared, I ran as fast as I could and caught myself on the lip of an open cargo car. I pulled myself in, but not without a moment of terror when my legs swung underneath and I thought I'd be pulled under and cut in half by the train wheels.

Once I was on the platform, I got into a kneeling position, ripped off my backpack, and turned around to see Jack falling behind. His legs and arms pumped furiously, his pack swung wildly on his back.

"Come on, Jack! Come on."

Jack tripped, lost his balance, and then righted himself. A flash of anger passed over his features, and then he threw out his hands. The air rippled, and the shockwave sent him shooting through the air. As I watched, he arced toward me, pinwheeling his arms. He hit me hard in the chest and bowled me over backward, back onto the train car's wooden floor.

When I got back my breath, I didn't know what to say. He'd just jumped thirty feet.

"Were you gonna leave me?" His voice was deceptively neutral. It didn't take a mind reader to know he was pissed.

"No. If you couldn't make it, I was gonna hop out."

"You were just sitting there."

"So? You made it didn't you? And how. You just jumped a freakin' mile."

The grouchy look remained for a bit longer, and then he smiled. "I did, didn't I?"

"Holy smokes . . . did you? Like a damned rocket. What's your superhero name gonna be?"

"Shut up."

"Mr. Explodey sounds good."

"Shut up."

"Maybe Jack the Frogman. No. Hopalong. Hopalong the jumping super-dude."

Jack looked like he was going to get all pissy, but then he laughed. "How about we call you Mr. Mysterio the Jerkwad."

"Nah." I buffed my fingernails against my chest. "I'm the Cannonball."

He looked puzzled.

"You know, because of my last name?"

"Huh. It doesn't fit, really. That's not what you do."

We fell silent, swaying with the movement of the cargo car.

When the train finally stopped, we were in Mobile, in the great state of Alabama.

■■■

The scam works like this. Jack takes the item to the cashier. It's usually something small, like gum or candy or the cheapest thing he can find in the store.

I tag along behind.

When the cashier pops the register, I go in. Not all the way. Not possessing. Just enough where I can change things, fiddle with what the cashier sees, play defense. While he's looking at Jack, he's not seeing me. It's a trick. A sleight of mind.

I can make someone look right through me. It's hard, but . . . desperation has shown us how strong we really are.

The bill Jack offers looks like a C-note instead of the single it really is. I can make that adjustment behind their eyes.

Some cashiers balk. Some ask where Jack got so much money.

It's his birthday, of course. He's a well-loved son of wealthy parents. Or sometimes it's a gift from Granny. Sometimes it's all Dad had in his wallet, and Dad's just around the corner.

Afterward, there's ninety-eight dollars and change in our pockets.

We work the coast. Mobile. Pensacola. Destin. Charleston. Moving east. Moving north.

We never hit the same spot twice. Two or three in a day and we've got meals, clothes, and our next Amtrak or

Greyhound ticket.

We're brothers. Any adult questions us, and Mom and Dad have just stepped away for a minute. Should we go get them for you?

If the do-gooders ask any more questions, I go in and get rid of them.

Gently. Always gently.

I don't use the trick on Jack. I don't peep his thoughts. But I've tried. And while my boy Jack is often physically motionless and silent, there's a roil of pain there, tumultuous and wild, that I can't penetrate. His thoughts are smooth as silk and hard as steel, and I can't get in.

I don't think he knows I've tried peeking. I hope he doesn't.

▪▪▪

Drugstores work the best. Acres of candy: Now and Laters and Twizzlers, Hershey's and Kit Kats and Mentos and Starbursts, Hubba Bubba and Wrigley's Spearmint—rank upon rank of sugar spun into multicolored toylike shapes. Unattended children are the norm—mothers and fathers distracted by their errand and duty—and something about a building with large amounts of drugs and people wearing what look like lab coats lends an air of safety and blinds them to the chief danger of leaving the kids by themselves. The pharmacy we're in, somewhere on the Alabama Gulf Coast, has high stamped-tin ceilings and a candy rack that goes on for miles under old-timey photographs of soda jerks and lines of servicemen drinking root-beer floats.

There are two brothers at the rack—real brothers—and as Jack and I approach, I can hear them talking softly.

"Lemme borrow some money," the blond one says.

"Hell, naw," the other, taller one, black-haired and wearing jeans, a New Orleans Saints T-shirt, and Chuck Ts, responds. "All I got is five dollars."

"Gimme a buck, man," the younger brother says, turning to face his sibling with a roll of Mentos in his hand. He's maybe twelve, the other fourteen. The tall brother has zits and wisps of hair sprouting all over his face. He looks like some Dr. Seuss version of puberty: oval head perched on a stalk of neck, thin ink-stroke beard hairs quivering in the air. The younger brother puts his head close and almost snarls, "Or I'll tell Dad about *you know what*."

I didn't know what, and for a moment I want to peep them to see what the hell they're talking about. But the face of the younger brother when he said *you know what* stops me, because it's a hungry animal face, a starving dog's snarl, a wolf's avid snout. This family ain't like the ones they show in Hollywood. But mine isn't either, I guess.

Jack's nudges me and nods at the comic book rack. He browses the pulp while I watch the two brothers.

They're well dressed, wearing nice shoes and shirts and jeans with logos proudly displayed. Healthy and tanned, even though the year grows late—they radiate wealth and prosperity.

The older brother digs in his pocket and pulls out a five-dollar bill. "This is all I've got. Gimme what you want."

The younger boy hands him the Mentos and then, as if he just thought of something else, he snatches a pack of Hubba Bubba off the rack and shoves it at his brother as well.

"That's more than a dollar!" Overmatched, elder bro takes the gum and stands, semi-defeated, and stares at the candy rack. Wolf-boy smiles, showing braces. He notices me.

His gaze takes me in very quickly, snapping from my face to my clothes to my shoes, *tick tick tick*. Wolf-boy sniffs.

I want to go in his head and see if he's rotten to the core, but I don't really want the stink of his soul on me for the rest of the day.

As much as I get into them, they get into me.

"Boys, it's time to go . . ."

Someone brushes past me, smelling of cologne.

"Oh, excuse me, son—" A tall man, dressed similarly to the boys, with a little figure on a horse swatting at something with a club on his left tit, moves past me holding a white prescription bag and stands by his two boys.

"You're not getting that right before dinner," the father says, looking at what the older son holds in his gangly hands.

"I've got my own money," Junior Seuss says, holding up his five-spot.

"Not the point, Brando. We're about to go to dinner . . ."

The father looks up and glances at me. He's dark-haired, too, like Junior, has a handsome, healthy face—lacking the wisps of hair and acne—like a piece of buttered toast. He looks at me, looks away. Looks back.

Suddenly I feel exposed, as if something in his glance is peeling away layers from me—not like Quincrux's mental assaults, not penetrating. Junior's glance was judgmental, dismissive. His father's isn't.

He watches me while Junior says, "Aww, Dad," and replaces the candy on the rack. I can't tell what Dad's picking up from me, but his face goes through a series of expressions and settles on a somewhat sad one, like he's seen a lost puppy or something. Which I am most assuredly *not.*

I feel the same anger bubbling up that I always felt, at Booth, at the penguins and suits come to preach at Casimir on Sundays, at the touchy-feely self-help crap Red Wolf ladles out to the fish. I want to wipe that smile from the man's face. I want to tear down whatever illusions of family or normalcy he has and expose him to my world, like ripping a scab from a knee. Why should he have beloved children? Why should those ungrateful wastes of space have a loving father? Why should they get such blessings while the rest of us scrabble and scratch to survive?

Furious, I go at the sympathy behind his eyes, as if it's some invisible organ in him and I am a surgeon. I am a lance. An arrow. A bullet. I'm going to make him see, I'm going destroy him and that sad smile.

The impact, when it comes, makes me ring like a bell, like a cartoon dog struck between two garbage can lids, vibrating to my core. He's like a rock wall, a steel door. Impenetrable.

I feel like I've been shocked, like I've pissed on an electric fence. I can't move, and I wonder what my face looks like then. Shell-shocked? Stunned? Plain old retarded?

Then something more strange and peculiar happens. Even though he's walled off behind titanium blast doors, even though I'll never read him, I can feel something in his mind shift, like tectonic plates rubbing together. Like a dragon rumbling and uncurling in a cave. Something in him awakes.

Something in him, something *not him* becomes aware of me. Looks at me from behind his eyes. Something riding him.

I feel cold, despite the heat of the day. My hair stands on end.

He's noticed something's changed. And his sons notice who he's looking at and turn to face me as well.

"Something wrong, son?" the man says. Wolf-boy grins. "You okay? You don't look so good."

I say nothing. Jack turns away from the comics to look at me, an alarmed expression on his face.

"Son? You okay?" The man takes two steps toward me and extends his hand as if to grasp my shoulder.

I blink and knock his approaching hand aside.

"Don't call me son. I'm not your son."

He looks confused now. "Of course not . . ."

It's so easy to go behind Wolf-boy's eyes. He's like a glossy magazine, and just as deep.

I point at the youngest. "He stole the school literacy week donation jar and bought a video game that he told you he borrowed from a friend. He buried the jar in the backyard, by the doghouse. You can find it there." I turn, moving my finger to point at the oldest. He's harder to get inside, maybe because he's older, or maybe because of the stricken look on his face like he knows what's coming. "And this one . . . this one . . ."

I see it all. The men's magazines under his mattress, the bottle of hand lotion. His slack-jawed and lascivious midnight masturbation sessions looking at men modeling skivvies.

I stop. No. I won't go that far. Now that I can, I don't want to destroy their life.

Family is like a fuse and bomb. Ultimately, even the best of them will blow.

The father starts and turns to look at his youngest. Wolf-boy says, "He's lying! I didn't!"

Junior Seuss looks like he's about to cry, and he's brought up his hands in a defensive gesture. But it's the anger coloring the father's face that makes me turn and run from the store, sobbing.

Jack finds me two blocks away, holding my head in my hands.

"What happened back there?"

I stay quiet, and he sits down next to me.

Eventually I say, "Sometimes it's all too much."

"What?"

"Everything. The world. Us. Me."

He nods as if he understands, puts his six-fingered hand on mine.

I guess he does.

▪▪▪

We stick to the shore to practice. It's a risk. We're in danger of Quincrux sniffing our trail. But we need wide expanses of water to get it down. To get it right.

Jack can fly.

Today we nabbed over a half grand working Charleston's tourist district. I hired a driver, and he brought us here, to Folly Island, nonplussed by the fact that two kids had so much cash. He gave me his card.

There's low cloud cover and a brisk wind. The beach is empty, wind-torn, and lined with dark buildings.

Jack's in skintight scuba duds we bought at a dive shop and swim goggles that make him look buglike and alien. It's gotten cold now, and the shore is chilly. I'm bundled up ten ways to Sunday, but I look forward to getting back to the condo.

When we arrived at Folly Island, dusk was gathering and cleaning women and maintenance men were coming in and out of the beachside buildings. Plucking key codes from their heads was easy.

The condo's got a large collection of movies, most I

haven't seen, and we brought a backpack full of dried pasta, soup, tuna, and jerky. It's the off-season, but if anyone shows I can get inside and make us invisible—at least for a little while. If there's more than one person . . . well . . . that might be tough.

"Ready?"

"Yeah. I'm ready."

"Listen, it's not the takeoff that's the problem. It's the touchdown. Your last one was sloppy."

That ticks off my Jack. He sets his shoulders at an angle, and I remember the Angry Kid statue. It seems my natural abrasiveness is what it takes to keep Jack unhappy enough to do his explodey trick on command. I'm fuel to the fire.

I pull up my knees and adjust my windbreaker.

"Remember, keep the anger pointing down. You got a raw deal. You got screwed. Get mad."

"Shreve, this isn't good. For me. For us. I don't know if—"

"You remember the witch? You remember what she did to you?"

Jack spits. Might be from a salty mouth of seawater. Might be just good old unadulterated anger. And that's what we need.

The witch always does it. That memory is still as raw in him as an open wound.

"You're above her. She's down there. Look down. You see? Remember what it felt like?"

He nods. His hair drips with briny water. The surf rushes in and recedes, the ocean ripping and tearing at the shore. It's beautiful out here, beyond the dunes, on the edge of the world. Even with our messed-up lives, it's hard to stay angry enough for flight.

So I try to get in. He's still steel. But I'm like acid, and I try to sear my way in. To corrode.

No dice.

I assault him. I batter him. But he slips away. I can't do it; he's still impenetrable.

"Hold the anger. Let it burn slowly. Let it out slowly. Do it. Go."

Jack runs at the surf, pumping his arms, building speed. He jumps, spasms, and then a perfect circle dimples the water below him. Jack rises ten, twenty feet into the air on a higher, faster trajectory.

"Again!"

He's pinwheeling his arms now, trying to keep upright.

"Now, Jack!"

He throws out his hands, palms down like his arms were wings, and he shoots upward. He rises out over the surf, over the waves, and into the blue of the Carolina night. Into the stars.

The higher he goes, the less effective his bursts. He's got nothing up there to push against except more air. I'm not stupid. I'm a troublemaker, but I used to listen in class. I know every action has an equal and opposite reaction.

Jack must have paid attention in that class too.

He's moving faster and out of earshot, what with the roar of the surf, when he wobbles and starts to roll. He's lost his balance. His head and torso tilt forward on an axis, like he's falling. Which he is, really. It's a controlled fall Jack does. A controlled plummet.

But then he does something I've never seen him do before. He throws out his hand in front of him and gives what I can only call microbursts—like an astronaut on a spacewalk. And his body rights itself. He puts his hands back in the wing position and rises on another explosion.

He's sixty or seventy feet up. If he gets any more altitude, when he comes down he'll break something. At that height, even water starts to hurt.

Jack starts his turn.

This is the tricky part. He throws his hands out to the left—bam—and he's turned his trajectory some, not much. Jack will never be a skywriter. He gives another burst to his left and one underneath to gain more altitude, and now he's flying parallel to the shore.

He's windmilling again, whirling his arms and pumping his legs like a runner, trying to stay upright. He's hit the apex of his last burst and is coming down now. He's not coming down too fast, but fast enough to smack the water hard unless he can stop himself.

He gives a buoyant half burst, and then another, slowly decreasing his altitude. Then he waits until he's ten feet from the surface and gives one last microburst upward. He tucks in his chin, puts his arms out in front of him in a dive, and hits the water.

I snatch up the towel and run to the point on the beach nearest his landing.

Jack takes a few minutes to swim back to shore. He wouldn't be able to fly if he wasn't such a good swimmer, that's for sure.

He's grinning when he comes out of the water.

"Nine point three." Our little joke. I score him on the landings.

"What? That's what you gave me, like, three weeks ago in Destin."

"Yeah, well, you were an amateur then."

I toss Jack the towel, and he dries off.

"Nine point five, at least."

"You were wobbly. But you did stick the dive."

We're both smiling now, amazed a human can fly. I don't know what genetics had to come together for this to happen, but it seems so improbable as to be magic. And maybe that's what it is. Maybe humans really have had magicians throughout history, and they were just kids with extra fingers and triple nipples and two dicks and abusive parents, surrounded by folks like Quincrux and the witch.

We turn to walk back up the beach.

"Race ya," Jack yells, dashing forward, and he gives a pulse that launches him fifteen feet in the air. He lands squatting, his feet digging deep into the sand and his arms out. But he rises fast and keeps running.

If he goes explodey, there's no beating him in the hundred-yard dash.

I'm left alone to trudge back to the condo.

▪▪▪

The old routines take hold. I'm used to cooking and cleaning and waiting on a younger brother. After hours of me bitching, cajoling, insulting, and assaulting Jack while he's doing the human rocket over the Atlantic, he's tired and needs to bring his core temp back to human levels. I'm happy to take care of things and let him warm up, wrapped in a blanket in front of the TV. It's been a long two months on the road, and most of the nights haven't been in digs as nice as this.

Tonight, Tuna Helper—Hamburger Helper's ugly sister—is on the menu. I've got some pickles to get some green on Jack's plate, but until we can settle somewhere, I don't see us hitting the local farmers market. We eat what we can tote in our trusty backpacks.

The condo is a glorified hotel room with a combination-lock door. Everything has its place, but nothing is personal. It's a snapshot of what a vacation must feel like, full of pastels and shells and tropical birds that have no business being within a thousand miles of South Carolina.

I might be a kid, but I'm not an idiot. The condo is pure fantasy.

I bring Jack a bowl of the noodles and tuna, and he sniffs at it, takes a bite, and puts it on the coffee table in front of us. Like Vig used to get after a long day of play, he's too tired to eat, but he'll be ravenous in the morning. Now he's watching the flickering lights of the TV, some stupid sitcom with impossibly pretty people; lights are on, but nobody's home for both Jack and the show. I could try and get in, to root around in his noggin, but I don't want to be that guy who takes advantage of you when you're down.

Friends don't do that. Brothers don't do that.

"Come on, bro. Let's get you into bed." I drag Jack up by the arm and march him to the bedroom. He puts up no resistance.

The condo has three bedrooms—two masters and one bedroom for kids, with bunk beds—and this last room seems the most appropriate for us. I'm not going to take a master and put Jack in the other. What if the landlord or owner shows up? And I'm not going to sleep in the same bed as him.

Bunk beds make sense.

Jack falls into the bottom bed. I pull covers over him, and he turns on his side, fully asleep. I pad back to the TV room, eat the rest of his Tuna Helper, brush my teeth at the kitchen sink. I open the front door and check the fenced atrium where we found the maids and I took the code from their heads. I check the patio door that leads out to the scrub grass and sand and dunes and the sea beyond, which even now I can hear like a dull roar.

I lock the door as much as it can be locked and turn back to the bedroom. Climbing to the top bunk, I imagine being back in Casimir Pulaski. I imagine being back in my bunk, letting the cold air coming from the vent cover me like darkness, and I close my eyes.

Where is Vig now? Where is Coco?

I keep my eyelids closed, moving my eyes in their sockets like I am seeing Little Rock from a bird's-eye view. There is Casimir, locked in chain-link and razor wire in the eastern section near the river port. And then, away there, off to the west at the foot of the Ozarks, Holly Pines.

I'm picturing this in my mind, and I rise up and away. Now I'm really rising, and I can feel Jack's presence below me like a frozen man can feel the radiant heat of a fire even from a distance. Jack and I are connected by a thin, bright filament—like a piece of gum you've chewed and then held between your teeth while you stretch out a piece until just the slightest tendril connects the gob in your hand to the one in your mouth. That's how the filament connecting Jack to me feels—wispy and thin, but there—except it's a filament of fire. A connection of gold.

And then I see the other, fainter filaments spanning away from me off to the west. I'm suddenly reminded of when Marvin, that giant among prison guards, tased me and I entered him through the wires shocking me, my awareness becoming electric.

So I follow these golden threads of fire. Over dark landscapes and the swell of the unknowing, massive ocean, over cities and fields and woods, I follow this fine thread of flame like a firebird on a highway in the sky. All I can think of is Coco. Leaving without being able even to talk to her broke a part of me that I'll never be able to repair—not by words, not by deeds. Or maybe that part of me died bleeding out into the cab of Billy Cather's truck.

I follow the filament until I reach a core brightness, and then I'm suffused with memory. I see Coco, hair golden and laughing, in the piney woods—caught in a ray of light streaming through the canopy of trees. I'm caught in her kiss, and I feel myself dissolving.

I can feel her. I know her. I am her. She is me.

Vig.

I stretch out and race down another thread, keeping Vig held in my mind like a lifeline.

He's warmer, fierce and stubborn and unhappy. When I join him, he fights me and pushes me away. But I surround him, and finally his spirit sighs and allows me to enter it. My little dude, so far away and all around me.

He's hurt and alone, like all of us, and he doesn't know I'm there.

I rise, and now I can see the filaments stretching away from my body. Thousands of filaments, golden and uncountable, connecting me to everyone I've ever met and ever might meet. I feel an instant of mind-numbing fear, because this is real. This is real. Whatever Quincrux did to me, even inadvertently, has left me open to this. I'm a puppet suspended over a vast abyss, webbed in billions upon billions of fiery threads. I rise, and I can't tell whether the billions of threads piercing me lift me up or whether I'm pulling them. The mesh that connects me to everyone and connects everyone to me becomes so massive in my mind's eye that I think my consciousness might be snuffed out like a tiny candle. How can you bear knowing that we're all one tissue? How can you live with that knowledge, knowing what your fellow man can do?

I pull and tear to rip myself free, sending tremors out along the threads like a fly caught in a web.

I'm everything my mother said I was. Selfish. I'd give anything to be back with Coco and Vig. I don't want to do this anymore. I want to give this all up; I want to go home.

And then I feel the coldness.

I want to close my eyes to the cold, but that's impossible now because eyes are for those who remain incarcerado. I've gone out into the wild blue yonder; I've gone out into the beyond. And while the mesh of humanity keeps me tethered, I feel a great, seeping cold—a darkness growing along with my expanding perception.

And then I'm high above the plane of threads and points of light, as though I'm standing on the peak of a mountain. To the north is the darkness like a black hole. I look that way and see a spot devoid of light, bare of the fine mesh of life and love and happiness. I see nothing but darkness there.

I think it might be Maryland. Where we're going.

Suddenly I'm terrified. I'm terrified that Quincrux and the witch might be traveling these same threads; I'm terrified that the darkness might perceive me. I'm terrified I'll be lost and never find my way back home. I squirm. I struggle. I writhe and rip and thrash, grasping for that one thread, that one brighter than all the others. Finally I seize it. I flee back down its length, and then I'm gasping.

I'm in my body, back incarcerado. It feels foreign to me now; I've been so far away from it and been so many other people. I sink in, and there's an instant, like in a heart transplant, when I think my body's going to reject me. Just a moment and then I'm in, gravity-bound and gasping for air.

Jack still sleeps below me. But when I close my eyes I can feel the pull of humanity, feel the pull from a billion filaments of fire.

I lie awake for what seems like hours but could be minutes. There's no telling time now that my perceptions have been so skewed.

Finally, I close my eyes and make myself fade to black. Releasing my grasp on consciousness feels like drowning.

FOURTEEN

Making the train attendants not see us is easy enough. It's such a little adjustment, really, I don't even have to go all the way in. Just a smidge to make them look elsewhere, past our seats to the next row.

I just have to go in with a crystal-clear picture of empty seats in my mind. And hold it.

And hold it.

While the other mind's owner scrabbles and squirms to get back in control, confused as to what's happening but not about to believe he's being invaded.

It'll wear a person out. Me. Or the target. It doesn't matter.

The single-to-hundred scam is easier by far.

The thing is, every person thinks he's imaginative and strong-minded. Very few people really are. I'm not excluding Shreve Cannon, magician and man-about-town, in that statement.

Most people are imaginative by reference; their fantasies are powered by images they've seen in movies, read in books. Most people couldn't keep someone like me, or Quincrux, out for more than a second. If Quincrux comes a-calling, he's going to get in. The dude is a monster. A demon.

I guess that's what I am. Quincrux, the witch. And me. Demons in human skin.

Not what I dreamed about as a career path. But I guess juvie wasn't much better for job prospects. And this pays better.

The train rocks sideways beneath us. It's strange and wonderful to me that Jack and I barrel down the track at fifty, sixty miles an hour to an uncertain future, but the only motion I can feel is the sway of the cars, left and right, contrary to our forward motion.

Jack's leaning against the window, eyes closed, and we pass through industrial parks and then woodlands and plains and fields and then city once more. The light from the sun is pale and yellow, coming in dappled flashes. It illuminates his body then casts it into shadow at a frequency of a failing fluorescent light bulb submerged in molasses. I can see his hands clearly, each finger, and his sleeping form reminds me of pale and bleached statuary at the state museum. A statue of the Angry Kid at rest. But the sculptor screwed up on the hands.

Hands are always the hardest part to draw.

Jack needs his rest. I close my eyes.

▪▪▪

We were in a brokedown little town in the Florida panhandle called Chattahoochee when I first possessed someone, full Exorcist. I was desperate.

The bus hissed to a stop at a brown, weathered concrete Greyhound station near a strip mall with forlease signs decorating the windows. The parking lot was littered with trash and empty bottles, smelling of yeast and motor oil. Jack gave me a concerned look as we exited the bus. It wasn't hot this late in the year, and the sun was low in the southern sky, bracketed by pines and nearly hidden by a tree line laureling a trailer park. Dogs barked, and the bus chuffed and ratcheted behind us as we walked toward the sad, squat motel on the corner beneath the yellowed sign that read Stay-Inn! above a lit vacancy sign. It reminded me of home.

After ten hours on the bus we were tired, and it was such a dump of a town, I thought we could rest there, at least for the night.

The door gave a little electronic beep as we entered the Stay-Inn! Motel lobby, where there was a single old man at the counter, legs kicked up and reading an *In Style* magazine. Checking out the celebrity fashions, no doubt.

Spying us, he dropped his feet to the floor, and his chair gave a little squeak of outrage as it shifted position beneath him. "Howdy, folks." Scrabbling at his mind, I was broadcasting a hundred thousand watts of pure, unadulterated young male imagery, stubble, big muscles, Adam's apples. Deep voices. Bull-like levels of testosterone and adulthood. Grave and serious. The full nine.

Approaching the man, Jack smiled and placed one of his hands on the counter. He said, "We'd like a room for the night. We'll pay in cash."

I don't know if I didn't have the illusion together enough, or it was Jack's hand on the counter, but the old man's eyes went wide, alarmed.

"I, I—" he stammered, and his gaze shifted to me and then back to Jack and then to Jack's hand lying there for the whole world to observe and count digits.

For one instant the old man looked absolutely terrified, face white and mouth loose so that his dentures lifted a little from his bottom jaw and his cheeks went slack and empty.

"We'd like a room," Jack repeated, and I almost yelled at him to shut up, because something was so very wrong.

Then a strange look came over the old geezer, like someone had flipped a switch in his noggin, and his face went blank. He slowly turned to the phone next to his reception computer, picked up the handset, and began to dial. A long number.

My heart hammering in its cage of ribs, I reached out to Jack and grabbed his shoulder.

"This isn't good, man. We've got to—"

In a dead, monotone voice, the old man said into the receiver, "Yes. Visual confirmation. They're here."

Jack stepped away from the counter, and the look of pure terror on his face was electric. Things seemed to slow and gel around us: the air became thick, and heavy motes hung in the low light streaming through the windows from the parking lot.

Inside I was screaming, "RUN!" but my feet seemed locked in place and Jack frozen into statuary.

The old man shuddered and closed his eyes, the phone held still held to his ear. When he opened them again, he was smiling. A familiar smile. A how-good-it-is-to-see-you-again smile.

"Ahh. Mr. Graves and Mr. Cannon. You've led us on a merry chase, but all that has come to an end." The voice was familiar even through the sputum and clatter of the old man's dentures. Quincrux, *here.*

I forced myself to move, grabbing Jack and spinning him around. "Run!"

The door's electric chime dinged, and we turned to run.

A big trucker of a man, shirt-tight barrel of a belly over a silver rodeo belt buckle, stood in the doorway, coming forward, sun behind him. For an instant I thought he might be one of Quincrux's slaves, possessed by the man, but he drew up short and gave me a perplexed look.

"Y'all okay, in here? You look like you seen a . . ." His eyes widened as he looked past us, toward the hotel register. I can't help myself. I looked back, over my shoulder.

The sight of him locked me in my tracks.

Blood poured from the old man's nose onto his clothes. It spread like a crimson oil slick across his mouth and chin and splattered on his shirt—*plat plat plat*—giving him a rapacious, hungry look. The old man at the desk said, "*Do not run.* I will have someone there in a moment to collect you. If you continue this foolish running, people will get hurt." He tapped his chest. "This old carcass. And the other watchers I have waiting for you. So many watchers. They will not fare well. Nor shall you."

The old man leaned forward as if he were reaching for something, head down. When he raised it again, he had a pistol in his hand.

"Or this unfortunate soul."

Freed, then, as if I'd pulled myself from quicksand. Everything happened at once. Jack and I leaped towards the glass lobby doors while the big belt-buckled man said, "Hey, wait a sec . . . ," raising his hands.

I ripped the door open as Jack flashed through the entrance toward the parking lot, and I was directly behind him as the boom and burst of light went off behind us like lightning and thunder and the air turned to shards of glass and a billion liquid particles of blood hanging immobile around us. Jack windmilled his arms wildly, his dark hair caught in a wild spray, his hands open like two fans, both legs extended, one in front, one behind, a wild look on his startled face.

Then everything snapped back, and Jack's foot came down on the concrete of the walkway and we were hauling ass out of there, into the parking lot, across the strip mall and into the trailer park and beyond.

It was a young woman, chewing gum, who stopped her car in the middle of the street as I waved her down. She was blonde and had tired eyes and a Motorhead T-shirt, looking at us quizzically, saying, "You boys need some help?" when I went in full-bore like a bulldozer behind her eyes, took her over and booted her out like I'd done to poor Marvin. I walked her body over and away from the car, onto the scraggly lawn of a pillbox home and sat her down cross-legged on the grass. Her nose was bleeding.

No better than Quincrux.

I pushed Jack inside the car, jumped in the driver's seat, and let the girl go. But for that second, that one instant, I felt like there was gum on my shoe, gum on my sole—my *soul*—and parts of me were stuck to her.

She was wailing, once again herself, as we pulled away.

▪▪▪

We ride north. Another city, another state, another place where we don't know anyone. And where no one knows us. And most important, where there's no Quincrux. He's out there, waiting. Every person we come into contact with could be a watcher like the motel attendant. One of the little toy soldiers Quincrux has scattered about the earth, programmed to spring into action once they see us.

It doesn't make me feel very generous to my fellow man.

On the outside, every face can hide a monster.

I haven't mentioned this to Jack, but I think he knows and we'll have to talk about it eventually. But not yet. Like a regular family, we have uncomfortable subjects we keep locked away in closets and under rugs. Under mattresses, like Wolf-boy's older brother. I worry that Jack, when we get right to the nitty-gritty of the matter, might go off into his own private wonderland, that faraway gaze seeing other times and places.

Gods, poor Jack. I think he sees a crib. A burning house. How can someone live with that?

I think about my vision of the filaments connecting us all. I guess it was a vision. I don't want to think about it. I don't want to be open to something that strange.

If it was real, then there's some bad stuff waiting for us up north.

▪▪▪

The first hotel we find, I can't get behind the receptionist's eyes. I come at her from every angle, but no dice. She's not as smooth as Jack, but she's just as impenetrable—like craggy, porous rock. Wolf-boy's father had been as defended, or more. He was steel to her rock. What are they feeding these people up here?

I feel like a dragonfly spattering itself against a windshield, going at her like that. I don't have time to wave Jack away before he steps up and starts the scam.

He holds out his library card.

"What is this?"

"We have reservations, under . . ." He glances at me. "Horace Booth."

"This isn't a library, kid. It's a hotel. And you've got to be at least eighteen to check into a room." She glances at me. I'm trying to crack her noggin like an egg. But it's not egg-shelled. It's stone.

"What are you two trying to pull here? Where's your mom? Your dad?"

Jack's not stupid. Those are words he's learned to fear.

"Just kidding!" Jack chirps and dashes off across the lobby. I follow. The woman stares at us, shaking her head and reaching for a telephone.

There's no percentage in waiting around to see who she's calling. I run hard, pumping my arms, right on Jack's heels. He's a fast little dude, Jack is.

We're down the street in a flash, taking the first turn we can find and throwing ourselves against the wall in a caricature of fleeing heroes.

"That was close."

"What happened?"

"I couldn't get in."

"What do you mean?"

"Her head. I couldn't get in. She was too strong. Like you."

Jack thinks about this for a moment. Then he says, "Well, I guess we better try again."

I sit down on the curb, between cars.

"What are we doing?"

"What do you mean? We're trying to get someplace to stay."

"No." I put my head in my hands. "I mean what are we doing here?"

Jack sits down next to me, saying nothing.

I sigh. "I'm just tired of moving. Quincrux's watchers could be anywhere. We can never know. We'll never be totally safe." I bite my lip and then say what we'd been trying to ignore since Chattahoochee. "He shot that trucker. Killed him just to force us to stop."

"We didn't pull the trigger," Jack said.

"No, but we could've saved him."

Jack shakes his head. "No, that man was doomed the minute he saw us. And Quincrux. How did he do that?"

"What?"

"Get in the old clerk. It's like he programmed the old man to look for us." He cursed softly under his breath. "You see how he never put down the phone? Creepy."

I want to explain that Quincrux could open the hood of anyone and tinker around inside. "Maybe Quincrux had to have some sort of connection with the guy to keep control."

"Maybe. But how did the old guy know us?"

"It's like when he commanded me to not remember. For some people, it's like a mental computer virus he's left behind, maybe. Quincrux plants one of *his* memories, and when they see us, recognize us . . ."

"The program activates, doesn't it? Oh god."

We will never be safe.

I leave that unspoken between us. Jack knows. I know.

Nothing left to do but run and hide. "We need to find a beach town where we'll be somewhat anonymous and settle down."

Jack shakes his head. "We can't, and you know it. The longer we stay someplace, the more likely Quincrux will find us."

"We don't know that, really. We don't know anything about him, or the witch. We don't know what they want or who they work for. Or how much money or power they have in the real world."

"We know they've got enough power to control people. If they can read minds, they'll find us."

I don't reply. He's right, but I'm tired of running.

"I had a vision last night."

That just popped out there. My mouth moves in mysterious ways.

Jack looks at me like I'm some kind of deep-sea creature floating to the surface, gelatinous and strange.

"Don't look at me like that, man. I didn't ask for any of this." I tap the fingernail of his sixth finger. "Just like you didn't ask for it."

I go ahead and lay out what I saw. Finding Vig and Coco. Seeing the black hole to the north. The bad vibes I got from it.

"I wondered why you weren't as eager to get to Maryland, why you bought us tickets to here." Jack looks at me sharply. "We're landlocked, you know. No practicing."

"Yeah. I'm sorry. I just . . ." I don't know how to say it other than just to say it. "I got scared. It's black to the north. There's no human light. No indication of . . . of the illumination of people."

Jack looks at me in the watery, unwavering way he has. Not judgmental, just considering. And waiting.

"Whatever is up there . . . whatever is causing that great black hole . . . it nearly killed Quincrux. And whatever I've learned, I'm nothing compared to him. So, yeah . . . I'm scared."

Again, silence. We stay that way a long while.

"Well, we can stay here for a couple of days." Jack claps an over-fingered hand on my shoulder. "But we've got to find somewhere to stay, and it's getting late. How much money do we have left?"

We have maybe three hundred dollars.

"Why don't we hit a few stores before they close and then try another hotel," I say. I look down the street. This part of Raleigh is crowded with big office buildings interspersed with motels, hotels, and chain restaurants. The sun slants in the afternoon sky, giving trees and buildings a warm haze even in the cold. In a couple hours it'll be dark. It's easier to make folks see what I want them to see when it's dark. I don't know why.

"Sure," Jack says. "Let's make some money."

We cross the road, navigating the traffic, and enter the Kwik Mart. The store smells like incense, tobacco, and stale beer. Jack grabs a pack of gum and a couple sodas, puts them on the counter. The cashier, a fat, hairy biker with full sleeve tats, is wearing a T-shirt emblazoned with a gigantic black raven. He turns away from a small television blaring wrestling and raises his eyebrow at Jack.

I go in, a full dive. It's like diving into a pool and finding all the water has been drained. It's like slamming into a brick wall, his mind is so strong.

Jack holds up a one-dollar bill, like we've done so many times before.

"That'll be three twenty-nine."

Jack's face clouds, and he glances at me.

I make another run at the biker, giving it all I've got. For a second I feel like I'm slipping behind the curtains, beyond the veil of sight. But I hear a buzzing, and then . . . inexplicably . . . I sense tectonic plates shifting, and something massive stirs, uncoils. A presence.

I think of Wolf-boy's father in the pharmacy, his head like a steel door.

During my vision I was suffused by Coco, by Vig. This feels like I'm witnessing someone—or something—suffuse the biker. Blackness pushes in on the edges of my vision, and my arms break out in goosebumps. I shiver.

The biker glances at me, blinks, and then turns back to Jack.

"That ain't gonna cut it, son."

Jack sheepishly pulls out more money, takes his change, and we leave.

"Don't."

"What?"

"Don't ask. I don't know what happened in there. Something is wrong. I felt—"

"Your nose is bleeding."

"What?"

I dig a handkerchief out of my backpack and wipe up the blood. It's just a little. Not too much.

Did the ability wear off? I felt like Quincrux opened a door in my mind, but could it have been temporary?

Could I have lost it? The idea scares me. And thrills me. To be just a kid again. That's something . . .

"Wait a sec."

I turn around and go back into the store. The burly man glances up from the wrestling and raises a caterpillarlike eyebrow.

"Excuse me, sir."

"Yeah?"

"Can I ask you a question?"

"What is it? Can't you see I'm busy here?" He gestures at the little TV set perched beside the register, nestled in among the cigarettes.

He doesn't look particularly busy to me, but he looks crotchety enough that I'm not going to push it too far.

"Just one question. Are you from Maryland?"

"No. Born in Philly."

"But your shirt . . ."

"Yeah. Lived in Baltimore for a couple months last year with my old lady. Edgar Allen Poe's two-hundredth birthday or something like that. What's it to ya?"

"Oh, nothing. Just settling a bet with my brother."

"Well, if there was money on it, you gonna split it with me?"

I laugh, because that's what it feels like I should do. After a moment, the biker laughs too, his bearded face splitting into a craggy grin. I wave and go back out to where Jack's waiting on the sidewalk.

"He lived in Baltimore last year."

Jack opens his mouth and then shuts it. He gives me a look like he's waiting to hear the rest. Quite the nonverbal communicator, he is.

"Baltimore is in Maryland, Jack."

"I know that. So?"

"I think there's some kind of connection between Maryland and not being able to . . . you know . . ."

Jack doesn't like talking about my abilities. He might be as ashamed of what I can do as he is of his hands.

"How could that be? I mean, why would that prevent you from doing . . ." He waves his hand in the air. "Your thing?"

"For a second I felt something weird. Like he had a rider."

"A rider?"

"Someone was already occupying the space where I was trying to go. Or something."

Just saying it gives me shivers.

"Hold up. Or something? What does that mean?"

"I don't know. When I got a little bit in, it just felt . . . foreign."

I can't really express what happens when I go inside someone, and Jack can only understand the shockwaves he can generate and his many, many fingers. All this mentalist stuff bothers him, it's so removed from the body.

His understanding is locked up. Rooted in the flesh.

Incarcerado.

I sigh, put my hands on my hips. "Just trust me, man.

Someone—something—else was there. Not controlling, just riding in the background. Watching."

Jack's quiet, looking at me closely.

Eventually he says, "I don't like how you say that."

"I don't know what to tell you, man. I didn't get any warm and fuzzies from whatever it was. That's all."

"I'm thinking we don't need to go any closer to Maryland."

I remember Quincrux's conversation with Ilsa. How he said at full strength he could make the whole yard of Casimir, all of the boys there, kill one another if he wished. The more I know now, the more I believe him. But he was recovering from the "incident in Maryland."

Now, if I were a hero, I'd set off trying to figure out what the darkness to the north is. I'd solve the mystery of the entity behind the biker's eyes. Behind Wolf-boy's father's eyes.

Screw that.

I should have realized that if Quincrux doesn't want to tangle with what's in Maryland, I sure as hell shouldn't get close to it. I fought Quincrux as hard as I could, and he cut through me like warm butter.

It doesn't take a mind reader to realize that going north isn't the best idea after all.

But we can't keep running forever. I just can't do it, squatting in condos, tricking hotel attendants into thinking we've got reservations and credit cards. I don't like it. I'd rather be back at Casimir. You know where you stand in juvie, and there's always a bed and three squares—which is more than could be said for even Holly Pines. For a moment I'm overcome with an intense anger at Jack, this kid who came and disrupted my sweet life there. It wasn't the best joint in the world, but it was safe, it was comfortable. I knew where I stood. I belonged there.

Ah, crap.

Jack's looking at me, head cocked and eyes wide, in the way that reminds me so much of my little dude. Of Vig. And my anger dissipates. Slowly. Slowly. But it goes.

"Maybe you're right." I'm quiet for a while, rubbing my chin. "We'll head back south. At least folks down there speak right."

He laughs, an easy laugh. I think back to what he was like when he first came to Casimir Pulaski. How locked off he was. How he would barely smile, or talk, or do anything. And now he's laughing.

We take a street to the right, backtracking, maybe one turn too early, heading back to the train station. Late afternoon now, light angled and beginning to turn golden. There's a nip to the air, and our hoodies are welcome. We pass a couple of blocks of pretty nice houses—nicer than anything in Holly Pines, but that ain't saying much—and up comes a chatter and hollering of voices. Boys' voices, teens maybe, not far away.

Jack looks at me, and I shrug. "Let's check it out."

Take a turn on the next block and there's a small empty lot, brown and green and golden in the light, with a handful of boys and girls—teens and younger—swarmed in the dust tossed from their restless feet on the sneaker-packed dirt.

"Here they are," the largest boy, easily my height, calls. "Now we got even teams!" He hefts a Wiffle bat and whips it around in an excited circle. "Come on, guys!"

I grin at Jack and he returns it, shucking off his back-pack and leaving it on the ground, and the other kids don't realize they don't know us until we're standing among them and pulling back our hoods.

"All right," says the largest and obvious chieftain of the kids, "Now that Phil and Greg are here . . ."

"That's not Phil," says a girl. Smiling funny as she says it, as if she's in on the joke. I wink at her.

"Huh?" Chief spins around, looks at us. "What the . . . ?" He scans the road, the neighborhood, and looks back at us. "Who're you?"

"Shreve. That's Jack. We're new in the neighborhood."

"You guys play Wiffle?"

I snort.

His eyes narrow, but with everyone lined up, looking at him, the light failing, he shrugs and says, "Okay, Shreve. You guys are in. You know the rules, but we play that you can bean somebody for an out. If you miss, the person can run it home."

"That's cool." We played a similar variation at home.

"You hit the Stevensons' roof? Auto homer. First team to ten or dark." He points with the long Wiffle-ball bat at a nearby roof and then whips the bat in another whistling arc.

A small lot in a small neighborhood with regular kids. Sunlight failing. Motes in the air. Jack smiling. A woman's high-pitched voice carries through the air, bright and piercing. "Daaaaannnneeeeee!!!"

"Shit, Chuck. She's calling for me," one kid says.

"Ignore her."

A good-looking blond kid scuffs his sneakers in the dirt and says, "She has to come lookin' for me, she's gonna be pissed. Let's hurry this up."

"Aubrey, you pick the other team."

A red-haired girl moves to stand beside Chief. They divvy up sides. Jack and me being the last two kids picked, we're on different teams.

The white Wiffle ball makes wonderful *thocks* as we hit it into the air, burning worms, skanking the fences. In the gathering dark Jack laughs, and I laugh with him, running as hard as hell and tossing the ball around. These kids are cool—nice kids. Aubrey asks me where I go to school, and I chuck my head from the direction we came from. "Malbey Fields?" She smiles. "Me too. You have Mrs. Crotchet, yet? She's a fucking doozy."

"Not yet." Chief pitches and the kid at bat clocks one, up high, and I dash to the fence and snatch it out of the air. "Booyah!"

We play. So easy. I feel like my body has become lighter, buoyant. There's one kid back in the "outfield" watching each batter like we're in the major leagues, and

I can hear him saying under his breath, "Short's the best posish they is . . . they is . . ." over and over again.

Jack's up at bat, hefting the yellow implement of Wiffle destruction. Chuck does his windup routine, pitches a couple of woofers, which Jack swings at anyway. The kids yell out the strikes as they happen.

Jack connects with the next one, the white ball making a hollow *twhock!* as it peels off to the left, falling outside of the baseline, and the group, almost as one, yells "*Foul!*" and Jack rehefts the bat.

It's then that one of the kids, Danny whose mother is waiting on him, says, "Holy shit, guys, he's got six fingers on his hand."

Silence. It's so out of the blue, no one says anything, and Chuck, who must not have heard, pitches the ball. Jack doesn't swing. His face has gone slack except for the pain around his eyes, and his shoulders hitch high, as if he expects a blow instead of the pitch.

The ball hits the ground in a puff of dust and rolls away. No one goes to get it.

Jack drops the bat.

"Shit, seriously. You see that? Hey . . . you." Danny begins walking toward Jack, and I intercept him.

"Back off, man. None of your business."

These kids look at me, and I'm struck for a moment because I thought I'd see anger or hatred on their faces. Or loathing. There's just interest, curiosity. Jack is new.

This isn't Casimir, and these kids aren't the general pop.

I look at Jack. "We better go, man"

We're putting all these kids at risk. Quincrux.

But secretly I'm thinking, *Damn you, Jack. Goddamn you for being so different. Couldn't we have just had this one afternoon?*

I'm ashamed at my anger with him. Moms was right. God, how I hate her for being right.

Luckily, at that moment Danny's mother calls again, and the sun is down and the Wiffle ball game has ended. A few kids, uninterested in the physical anomaly amongst them, take off for home. Chuck picks up the bat and ball. Danny stares hard at Jack even though his mother is calling and finally says, "That's cool, man." He waves and takes off, calling over his shoulder, "Nice to meetcha!"

We gather our backpacks, start to walk back towards the shops and drag just a few blocks away, when Aubrey trots up and falls in beside us.

"You're not really from around here, are you?"

I shake my head. Jack's got this vacant, empty stare—hollow as a Wiffle ball.

When I don't respond any further, she says, "Well, I think it would be awesome if you went to school at Malbey." She takes my hand. Hers are very warm. Slightly moist. "Your brother is cute. But I like my boys tough," she says and passes me the piece of paper. She's got brown hair and a narrow face, but her smile is easy and generous and there's a mischievousness to her stare that makes me warm and nervous.

She lets go of my hand and walks off into the dark, toward home.

Jack and I walk a few minutes more. I open the paper, look at it.

A phone number.

It's harder than I thought to throw it away.

▪▪▪

We decide to hit a few more stores and shops and see if I can work the scam at all. To make sure this thing that Quincrux gave me hasn't dried up. We walk south without even thinking. Away. Putting distance between us and . . . and . . .

It. The thing in the north.

But all the while I'm thinking, *Them. Between us and them.*

FIFTEEN

Another cashier with a noggin like titanium, and then our luck changes and we manage three in a row as easy as getting into as an unlocked car. I dive in and root around. Nice folks, regular lives, struggling to get by. They've all done bad stuff and had bad stuff done to them, but nothing out of the ordinary. It's not that I want to snoop, but I need to prove to myself I can still do it.

It's scary, but I've come to rely on my ability. I guess Quincrux didn't realize he was giving me a gift when he was possessing me. But if I had my way, I'd rather he'd never come to Casimir.

I can't say the same about Jack. And with Jack comes Quincrux. It's a sad truth that I won't linger over.

When our cash flow is back up near a grand, it's late, nearing ten. And the later it gets, the more nervous I get, worrying about local curfew laws. They say the freaks come out at night.

And here we are.

We grab a cab and head back to the Amtrak station, the second time today.

By the time we roll out of the cab, the downtown

Raleigh streets are semi-deserted. I realize as I'm staring up into the buzzing, lonely streetlight outside the train station that I don't even know what day it is.

Jack looks dazed. He's got his thumbs hooked in the straps of his backpack like some farm boy snapping his suspenders. His fingers are fanned wide and on display for any Tom, Harry, or Dickhead to come along and see.

"Jack." I toss my head in the direction of all those fingers pointing everywhere. "Hey, man. You're a bit conspick."

"Huh? Oh." He stuffs them in his pockets and blushes.

"Listen, bro, we're gonna get a sleeping car. It'll be more expensive, but we're flush now and the farther away we get, the easier it'll be to get more. Right? We'll head down to Charleston maybe. Or Jacksonville? We'll be snowbirds or tourists, sunning ourselves on the way to Disney World. Whatdya say?"

"I liked Florida when we were there."

"Yeah. That sounds good. Maybe we can make it down to the Keys. Nothing to stop us."

He yawns. "Okay. That sounds fine."

When you're running, what direction you run in doesn't really matter, as long as it's away from danger. Of course, Jack and I couldn't even explain to you what we are running from.

We head into the station and buy Mountain Dews from a vending machine so we can get our systems a little more caffeinated for the transaction. I might have to alter our appearances. Technically, you can't buy tickets unless you're an adult and can present a valid form of ID. The rule is never enforced in our experience, though; we've bought tickets plenty of times without any kind of magic whizbangery from me. And there's the real trick: knowing when you don't need to do anything at all.

But whatever the case, I have to get inside and be ready to make adjustments if need be. Make the teller see college students rather than kids. Make him see a driver's license instead of a library card. Getting into someone's noodle takes energy, and I'm already tired from throwing myself against brick walls all day.

The ticket counters are in a row against the far wall. A guy sits behind a wire-crosshatched booth, looking out at the transients, derelicts, and travelers. He looks infinitely bored.

We approach, and I make the move once I can see the guy's face. I'm learning my power. I need to see a face for it to work. I've got to be pretty close to the target. I hate thinking about people that way, but there it is: I'm predatory. Better that than the alternative.

The counter dude is sallow-cheeked and a smoker. He's got greasy hair and an Adam's apple like Ichabod Crane's on a wattled, splotched turtle neck, long and crooked.

Jack has his wallet out and says, "Two tickets to Jacksonville, Florida, please."

And now it's time for me to go in.

The man is crusty on the outside. His insides resemble his outsides, his stream of consciousness slightly frozen over. But when I hit, it cracks and there's a hole through which I can enter. I dive under without much resistance.

And inside it's cold and strange. There are currents and eddies inside this guy that are as strong as the tides in oceans or the whirlpools in a sea. I descend into the depths, searching. It's foul and cold but fascinating, too, for the inquisitive mind. I can't help myself; I follow the pull of the waters, going darker and deeper. Down into the depths where there is no light and the pressure is near unbearable and the darkness is illuminated only by cold and foul things that give off their own sickly light . . .

"You'll have to change trains in Charleston. That'll be two seventy-five for both of you."

He takes Jack's money and gives him two tickets, still bored, still oblivious to my invasion. I'm struggling to come out of the depths of the man, to rise from the ocean of his thoughts and memories. I don't know if I can make it. In the end I just rip myself away. I rip myself out of the man. He jumps and maybe, just maybe, realizes something is amiss.

Jack's turning away as I start to retch, heaving up the sandwich and soda I had earlier, spewing it on the concrete outside the ticket counter.

"Hey!"

Jack looks at me with a worried expression on his face.

"Sorry, mister! My brother's sick."

I'm heaving now as Jack tugs at my arm and drags me away. I can only get myself under control once I realize that Charles Birch Dubrovnik might leave his booth and come after us.

"Go . . ." I stumble toward the train platforms, off-balance. Jack holds my arm and keeps me upright.

He leads me to our platform, train 213, platform 3, southbound. It smells of diesel and cigarette smoke and vomit. Maybe the vomit stink is coming from me.

"What the hell is going on?" Jack sounds exasperated and more than a little pissed.

The platform is near-deserted except for a couple of businessmen down the way and a derelict a few benches down. It's nearing midnight, and this should be the last train of the night.

"No, Shreve. I'm serious. What the . . . what is going on? This is like the third or fourth time today you've . . . you've . . ." He pauses, not knowing how to say it because he doesn't like the idea of what I can do. Poor baby.

I can't help the bitterness that creeps into my voice. "Hey, not everyone can just go explodey. Or fly . . ."

I can see it hurts him, but I don't care. He's hurt me.

Jack sits down next to me and puts his hands on his knees. He breathes deep, like he's trying to clean his airways.

"I've asked you not to call it that."

"Yeah? Well, get off my back. When you do your thing, you don't have to jump into cesspools. You don't have to lose yourself in . . . in . . . monsters."

His eyes bug. At least now I've got his damned attention.

"What monster? Quincrux?"

"No. We can't leave. We got to stay here now."

"What? Why?"

"That guy. His name is Dubrovnik. He's got a little girl in a secret room under his house."

Jack looks bewildered. He shakes his head, like he's trying to deny it. "Why would he do that? What's the point? I don't—"

"Why do you think, man?" I spit onto the concrete platform. My mouth tastes like bile and pecan shells, acrid and nutty all at once.

We're born into pain and we die in it, and along the way monstrous adults and horrible children do what they can to inflict pain on us because it pleases them. It gives them pleasure. Of all of them, Dubrovnik is the worst. He makes Ox and Quincrux look like angels. I got it all in the few moments I was inside. And I'll never be clean again.

Never.

Jack stays quiet for a long time, looking at me with a confused expression on his face. It's like he's seeing me for the first time, and I'm not really what he expected.

I'm not really what I expected either, bro.

"We can't leave. We have to help her."

"Are you sure it wasn't . . . I don't know . . . a false memory? A fantasy? He could be crazy."

I think about it. It's possible. But I don't think so.

"No. But even if it is, we have to find out."

"We don't. We can just leave. You know his name. You can call the cops, report him."

That's an idea. That's a good idea. "Okay. Let's do that. But we still have to stay."

"Why?"

"What if the police don't follow through? What if they don't find her? She's under the ground! Don't you understand? He forces her to do what he wants."

The derelict from down-platform stirs and looks at us. Another person who's seen us. Another breadcrumb along the trail that Quincrux could pluck up. Or maybe one of his buddies is already riding behind those eyes. Maybe we're as good as caught if we stay here another second.

Jack looks nervous and holds his hands out, trying to calm me. "Ssssh. Shreve, just—"

"It's like the witch but worse. A thousand times worse, Jack. She's just a baby. God, I wish you could understand. But god, I wouldn't want you to have to see it, what happens there. *Ever.*"

"Listen, Shreve, we've got to be cool about this." Jack grabs my shoulder. "Could it have been the . . . the thing you saw in the guy at the store?"

"The rider?" I shake my head. "No. Totally different. Listen, I'm no Quincrux. I can't . . . I don't want to possess people. I don't want this! But I know what I saw. That man is a monster. He's as inhuman a monster as you could imagine."

"But, how do you—"

I'm angry now. There's no denying it anymore. The voice of reason needs a smackdown.

I tear at Jack's mind, the hard obsidian exterior of it. I rip and fret, trying to get in. To show him.

And for a second, for just an instant, I get a foothold. I get in. And I make him see.

We dash away from here, this platform, hard and foul, out and away, down the rabbit hole. He sees what I saw. With Dubrovnik's hands we unlock the trapdoor in the basement. With Dubrovnik's feet we slowly walk down the steps into the raw, earthen room gleaming wetly, a single bulb in a caged socket throwing interlocking shadows on clay walls. And the bed and weathered mattress, stained and soiled, where she cowers. Where she waits, mold growing on her clothes.

I show him.

And then there's a wrenching, the air wavers, and I'm kicked out so hard I gasp. My knees go weak and reel from the eviction. I sit down hard on my ass and the breath whooshes out of me.

It takes me a moment to recover. I look at Jack, and he's not even the Angry Kid statue. He looks back at me with almost hatred. To save her, I had to break him. Just for a second—that was all I could manage. But it was enough.

God. What have I become?

"Never. Never. Do. That."

It's all he can get out. But now he knows. His shoulders slump, and he sits back down, hard, on the concrete platform. He holds his hands open in his lap. Counting the fingers maybe. I don't know. I hope he understands why I had to do it.

We sit there for a long while. I'm looking at Jack; he's looking at his hands. I'm holding my breath. I have nobody in this world except Jack. And now look what I've done.

Finally, when he talks, his voice is raw and tender.

"So we call the cops. Then we follow him home?"

"No. I managed to . . ." I swallow. I don't know if this will set Jack off or . . .

Jesus H.

"I pulled his address."

"Why us, Shreve?" Jack's not looking at me. Still. "Why does this have to fall to us? Hasn't . . . everything . . . been hard enough?"

Now he's just feeling sorry for himself. Don't get me wrong, I've felt the same way every day since we've been gone from Casimir Pulaski. Some people just can't stand to see someone feel sorry for himself. I'm not that person. Sometimes people deserve a little self-pity.

"I don't know." I pull out my wallet and check my funds. Three-fifty. Jack has the rest. We keep the money separated in case we get separated. "It's like asking why do dice roll a seven? There's no why to it. It just does."

Jack blinks his big brown eyes, wipes his nose, and then, finally, looks at me. I look back.

"I'm sorry about . . ."

He waves a hand like shooing a fly. He looks annoyed. "Forget it. You had to." I don't even have to scratch to know he's walled up tighter than ever. Maybe even the witch would have trouble getting in now.

He's different, my Jack.

"Well, if we gotta do it, we might as well start."

He stands, and I follow. There's a pay phone at the end of the platform. I walk to it. Take out some change and feed the slot until I hear a dial tone.

I dial 911.

"911, what is your emergency?"

I'm startled at the woman's voice firing down the line into my ear. It's all happening too fast, almost.

"A man. He's got . . ."

"Yes?"

Jack stands beside me at the phone. He leans in and puts his head against mine so he can hear the woman.

"There's a man. His name is Charles Dubrovnik. He's got a girl locked away in his basement."

There's a pause on the line. "How do you know this, sir?"

"I—" I didn't think this through well enough. "We were playing in the yard beside his house. We heard her screaming for help."

"Did you have any further communication with her?"

"No . . . just heard her screaming." I ought to try and add something. "We're not making this up. Her situation is . . . was . . . it sounded horrible."

Another pause.

"When was this? You were playing in the yard at midnight?"

"No, it was right before dark. It's just . . . we were . . ."

"Scared?"

I try to make my voice small. It's not too hard.

"Yes."

"Okay. What is the address?"

"5310 North Palm. Raleigh."

"We're dispatching a patrol car."

"A patrol car? Shouldn't there be . . . I don't know . . . like a SWAT team or something? I mean . . . he's got her in the basement."

"Your name, sir? Can we reach you at this number if we get disconnected?"

Man, I really didn't think this one through.

"Horace Booth. My name is Horace Booth. You can reach me here."

"Please stay on the line." I hear a click. Maybe she's recording this conversation for quality assurance.

I look at Jack, and I can tell from his expression he realizes we've got to move.

I'm so damned tired.

I say into the receiver, "Ma'am?"

"Yes?"

"I have to step away from the phone for a minute to use the bathroom. I'll be right back."

She makes a sound of assent. I very carefully lower the phone and let it hang by its metal cord.

We've got to run, again. On the bright side, our tickets will still be good tomorrow.

We head back up the stairs, but not before passing Dubrovnik's counter. He's not there anymore.

I hope he's just on break.

SIXTEEN

Palm Street is dark and hardly looks tropical. The neighborhood consists of row upon row of small, tightly packed houses. Far nicer than trailers, for sure, but still . . . older and a tad run-down. I see paint peeling in the yellow porch lights. Threadbare screen doors. Cars on blocks and collapsed wading pools that have lain there, forgotten in front yards, since summer. Very much like Holly Pines.

I'm guessing these little boxes house the city's workers, the people who man gates and sweep up at night, who teach public school and, possibly, guard wards of the great state of North Carolina.

I asked the cab driver to drop us off in the high four thousands of Palm, and he looked at us like we were crazy.

"Whatdya mean? You ain't got a fixed address or something?"

"No, we're just trying to surprise Mom."

"It's three in the morning. She'll be surprised, son."

"She's waiting for us."

"Whatever you say, kid."

There's another breadcrumb for Quincrux to follow.

Jack and I stroll down the sidewalk, trying to look like we belong here. But we're conspicuous this early in the morning, and we're both so tired it's hard to stand up straight. The sidewalk is rippled from tree roots, and I find myself stumbling more than once.

When we get to the fifty-one hundred block, Jack slows and sits down on the grass of a lawn between two privet hedges. It's hard to believe we started this day leaving the condo on Folly Beach. I guess it's not this day, technically. Yesterday.

I sit next to him but keep my backpack on. I lean back into it. The grass is wet, and dew seeps into my jeans. I can feel the coldness on the back of my legs and my ass. I'm too tired to care.

I'm about to speak when the lights grow. A car is coming. We pull back our legs so the hedges cover us.

When the car passes, I see it's just a sedan.

Not much traffic this late at night.

"We gotta keep moving, Jack. Gotta find Dubrovnik's house."

"How long's it been?"

"Since we called? I don't know. Thirty minutes maybe. If they've busted him, they'll still be there. You know, forensics and stuff."

I peek out from behind the hedge.

"I don't see any lights from cop cars. We've got to get closer."

He sighs and rubs his face. "Okay."

“Wait a sec.” The light is growing again. We stay put.

A police cruiser passes us.

“That’s it, Jack.” I stand. “Let’s go.”

I pull him up. I can see big black bags under his eyes, and I have to remind myself that Jack’s . . . what? Just thirteen? So young. But I guess I am too. I feel old now.

He squares his shoulders, and we start off again, doing our best to stick behind bushes, moving from shadow to shadow.

We trot down the two blocks until we can see the cruiser parked in front of a house. The house looks like all the others, except the yard is better tended, even this late in the year. Two very large crepe myrtles have been pruned back, making them look like the bones of some prehistoric, underground creature rising from the earth.

We cross the street, crouching low and running. I doubt it helps at all, running like this. It makes my pack bang against the small of my back and swing wildly, making more noise than if we’d simply walked quickly. But that’s how they do it in the movies, so there must be a reason.

Behind a truck in the driveway across the street we have a good view of Dubrovnik’s front door and the police cruiser.

A cop is framed in the light coming from the Dubrovnik house. He and Dubrovnik are talking, and I can see the flashing blue light from a TV inside the home.

I stretch out, send out my mind, and try to get inside the cop. But he's too far away.

They're talking, and Dubrovnik laughs, smiling wide. The cop drops his hands from his belt. His body shakes, and I realize he's laughing too.

"Jack, I've got to get closer."

"No. You can't help her if you're caught."

"I gotta see if I can make the cop—"

Jack grabs at me as I jump forward, running out and around the truck, toward the knee-high hedges at the edge of the lawn just before the sidewalk. When I hit the dirt, I look back at Jack. He's peering at me from behind the truck. Then he runs down the driveway, in full view. He jumps. He shoots through the air, thirty or forty feet, and then in the dark of the lawn across the street I see him land, hard, squatting on his hams. But he stands, no bones gone crunchy. I'm quite happy for him, the little leaper. Good for him, he doesn't have to violate people to save them.

Lying there, I smell the richness of the soil and the mulch around the hedges, and I close my eyes and try to center myself. It's not easy centering yourself. Now that I think of it, I don't even know what it means, really.

I open my eyes, raise my head, and spot the cop. I can't see his face, I can't see his eyes, but I have to try to get in.

I rush at him. His mind is as hard as diamond. He's lived in Maryland at some point. Either that or he's Quincrux's nephew.

Something arcs through the air, and I see Jack land on Dubrovnik's roof. Jesus. The kid is like Spiderman or something. But that's got to hurt.

The cop gives another laugh. Dubrovnik and the police officer shake hands, and then the cop walks back to the cruiser, gets in, and starts the engine.

So much for Raleigh's finest.

I can see Jack perched at the apex of Dubrovnik's roof, silhouetted against the early morning sky. He doesn't look like Spiderman now. He looks like a kid with a backpack on trying to balance himself on the peak of a roof. But something in his stance makes it different.

Maybe it's that he knows if he falls, he can save himself. A powerful thing, that—knowing you can save yourself.

Dubrovnik steps out onto the porch, that same sallow look even in the darkness. He lights a cigarette and watches the cruiser drive off. Then he remains on the porch, smoking, looking out into the night.

It feels like he's looking for me. I hug the earth. I kiss the ground, push my face in. I keep my mind silent.

I touched him earlier. I went in deep, and I know I could have taken control. I could have worked him like a puppet. I could have. But it was so foul there, so full of horrible thoughts and memories, I couldn't make myself do it. As much as I get into them, they get into me. I doubt if I could do it now if I tried. The truly scary thought I found is that Dubrovnik feels there's many things he hasn't been able to do yet. And while he knows what he's done is wrong, those thoughts are diffuse and abstract and he's not really concerned with the consequences.

He doesn't even know the girl's name.

And he doesn't care.

Eventually he snubs out his smoke under his heel and turns back into the house.

Jack leaps again, streaking through the air, away from me and behind the house. After a moment I see him caroming through the air again, pinwheeling his arms, and he lands with a heavy thud on the peak of the roof.

The porch light comes on again, and Dubrovnik comes back outside.

He walks into the yard and cranes his neck to look at the top of the house. Jack flattens himself against the roofing, moving downslope on the far side.

Dubrovnik, blinded by the porch light, seems to shrug and goes back inside.

Now we have to wait.

God, I'm tired.

▪▪▪

Before sunrise I find a bit of hedge far back from the road, secluded and out of sight from the neighbors and Dubrovnik. It's quite the prickly, uncomfortable seat, but I imagine Jack isn't faring much better on the roof. Despite the branches jabbing me in the back and scratching at my exposed skin, I manage to doze.

When I wake, the sun has crested the diminishing line of houses on Palm, and cars are on the street.

The neighbors whose yard I'm squatting in leave in two small sedans, the dad in slacks and a tie, the young kids squalling and complaining to their mother on their way to school. Damned ingrates don't know how good they've got it. If I had a family like that I'd . . .

Who am I kidding? I'd be just like them.

After a while the street quiets, the traffic thins, and the sun rises higher over the line of houses. I could fall back asleep in my bed of mulch, but I see Jack's head pop up on the roof and he points downward. I hear a faint clanking and clattering. Then the detached garage door rolls open and a dull brown station wagon, old and rumbling, rolls out and into the street and drives away.

Jack leaps. He arcs high in the air, keeping his arms out and palms facing down, and lands directly next to me on the lawn.

"Damn, man. You're getting good at that."

He lifts his foot and shows me the divots in the grass.

"I gotta get some cushier shoes. My feet are killing me."

"Are you slowing yourself in the descent?"

"Of course. Otherwise I'd have broken legs. There's no real way to control it without more practice. Just trial and error."

I wonder if the anger, the outrage, helps him. Dubrovnik hasn't helped my disposition any. I had bad dreams lying in the dirt. But I've never seen Jack as confident.

"You know what happens next, don't you?"

He snorts. "Yeah. We go in."

"Right." I wipe away the dirt and mulch sticking to my clothes. "So you can jump like the dickens, but can you still do your explosive thing?"

He gives me a sharp look. Then he holds up his hands like a surgeon. "Still me, Shreve. Nothing's changed. Just don't stand behind me. And if things look bad, hit the deck."

"Jack."

"What?"

"I'm sorry."

"About what?"

"Yesterday—at the train station."

"Forget it."

He knows what I'm talking about. If you're a mind reader, you don't have bad dreams without cause. Or maybe you always have them. Hell, I don't know.

"I had to."

"Didn't you say that already?" Jack shakes his head and spits.

Seems like me and Jack ain't best buds anymore. I don't know if that hurts more than having to leave Vig, but it's close. It hurts.

There's nothing for it except to do what we came to do. The police won't help. The girl can't help herself. Anyway, we're standing in the wide open, in the morning sun, and the conspicuous factor is rising fast.

"You check out the backyard?"

"Yeah. Patio, sliding glass door. Door to the garage."

"Whatdya think?"

"What? I don't know. You're the thief. You tell me."

I guess I deserve that.

"I think we should just blow down the front door, three-little-pigs style. Go in fast. Free the girl. Get out fast."

Jack's eyes narrow. He's thinking. "Yeah. Maybe so. Hold on."

He takes three steps and jumps, shooting into the sky and over the house.

A moment later Dubrovnik's garage door rattles up, and Jack waves at me from the darkness inside. I dash across the street.

"Unlocked."

Jesus H. Shoddy security for a monster.

For a moment I'm overwhelmed with fear: what if what I saw was just a false memory, a disgusting fantasy? I could be wrong. I'm new to this, and yesterday was exhausting. I could have screwed up. No monster would leave his back door open. He would guard it. Monsters have to hide, right?

Jack moves to the inner door. He puts his hand on it, looks back at me, and says, "I'm going first. Just in case."

"Hold on." I stop and take off my backpack. I dig out Marvin's Taser. "Okay, let's go."

Jack turns the knob, and we go in.

SEVENTEEN

It's a yellowing, shabby kitchen with patterned linoleum and flower-print wallpaper. It stinks of stale smoke.

For a moment I'm reminded of my mother's trailer. But where her home is trashy, this one is immaculate, despite the smoke smell.

I turn to Jack and whisper, "She's underneath the basement. He's dug a room."

"I remember." It's almost a snarl.

Right. I made him see. He's never going to forgive me for that.

"I have no idea how to get into the basement."

"Huh. We'll have to search."

Jack's calling the shots now somehow. I don't know whether that means we're near the end of our partnership . . . our brotherhood . . . or whether it just means he's in charge.

Why does everything have to be so hard?

We start opening doors. A utility closet. A pantry. A closet full of coats. Jack looks at me, shakes his head. He points. Moves on to the hall. A bathroom, then another closet.

Then, suddenly, a man is standing in front of us. He's a foot away from Jack, filling the dim hallway with his shadow. Dubrovnik. I know it's him, even though I can't see his face.

He swings something, and Jack jerks sideways, his head leading. The sound of the impact sounds like a branch breaking under the weight of snow, bright and resounding but wet too. A moist crack.

Jack hits the wall and slumps to the floor.

Dubrovnik steps over his body and advances toward me. Even in the dark, I can tell he's smiling. This is fun to him.

It's my job to make it not fun for him.

I raise the Taser and pull the trigger.

Two darts lance through the air and embed themselves in Dubrovnik's chest.

He doesn't jerk or fall or tense. Nothing. He just reaches up and yanks the darts out.

It's been more than two months. The charge is dead.

Never have I felt anger like I feel now. Not when Moms abandoned us. Not when I think about Billy Cather and being shot. Not when I think about a father who never was. The anger is like an explosion in my skull, and I'm not even trying to invade Dubrovnik's head.

I shriek and race down the hall at him, arms out, leaping.

He swings—a billy club, it looks like—but the walls are too close here. The tip bounces off a doorframe and hits me in the shoulder instead of the head. The pain is sharp but not unbearable. Unfortunately for Dubrovnik, I have a good head of steam, and inertia is a bitch.

I barrel into Dubrovnik, fists swinging. The first one clips him on the cheek, and his head rolls back. But he flings up an arm and blocks my left as he grabs me with a gnarled hand, unimaginably strong. I yelp as the bones in my left wrist grind together. A sound issues from his disgusting throat. It takes me a moment to realize he's laughing. It's a phlegmy, evil sound. But it's cut off as his feet hit Jack's inert body and he begins to topple. Backward. Taking me with him.

I bring up my arm as we fall. His head bangs on the hardwood floor, and my elbow smashes into his throat, hard. I feel the flesh of his neck and the gristle of his windpipe giving. I push down as hard as I can, shoving my forearm down like I'm bearing a shield, grinding it into his neck.

Dubrovnik begins to thrash. One of his big, gnarled fists catches me on the temple, and the world teeters and I see stars and I'm rolling away from him. When I get my sense of direction back, I spy the dull, blunt shape of the billy club—no, it's a miniature baseball bat—and I snatch it up and scramble to my feet.

Dubrovnik is gasping, his hands clutching at his throat. He looks at me with wide, terrified eyes. *Having a hard time breathing, are we? Let me help you with that.*

It doesn't bother me one bit that he's looking at me right in the face when I clobber him with the bat.

▪▪▪

"Fat lot of good all these superpowers did when he came at us," I say, glancing at Jack. He's woozy and unstable, and his scalp bleeds all over the place. He looks like a survivor of a terrorist bombing.

I take him into the kitchen and give him a glass of water. Then I grab a dishrag and mop up the blood oozing from his head. Once I get him on a kitchen stool, I search through all the drawers until I find some white nylon rope.

My head is a little woozy, too. I can feel my cheek swelling. I'm afraid the left side of my face will never be the same. First Ox smashing me into cinders, and now Dubrovnik. But at least Dubrovnik's going to roast for it.

I trudge down the hall to Dubrovnik's body. I check his pulse. Still here in the land of the living, the bastard. I yank his wrists backward, tie a tight loop around them, and then begin trussing the monster like a hog. Once he's bound tight, I go back and check on Jack. He's still just sitting there, gazing at the hideous wallpaper. It's patterned with birds and pears and what looks like a cherub playing a lute.

That's creepy, the cherub.

I've got to find the basement.

"Who was . . ."

Jack's voice is slurry.

"So, who left? Who was the person in the station wagon —"

"Hold on, man. I've got to find the girl, quick."

I race down the hall, throwing open doors. The one to the basement is the last on the left.

The stairs creak as I head down. I feel along the walls for a light. I can't find one.

It smells moldy down here, and the air feels dank and cooler than upstairs. After a few moments my eyes adjust to the darkness, and I think I can make out a lighter-colored line above me. I wave my arms above my head and, sure enough, hit a string. Once it stops swaying, I grab and pull and I'm blinded by the glare of the single hundred-watt bulb.

I've never been in a basement before, since trailers don't have them. But heck, all trailers have TVs. And this basement looks like what I think a basement should look like. I see a workbench and a wall of shelves holding preserves and boxes. The floor is concrete. A washer and dryer sit in the corner along with a treadmill.

What I don't see is a door to a sub-basement.

I search the concrete, looking into all the corners.

No door.

"Can you hear me?" I scream. "Can you hear me!"

I send out my mind, leave the prison of my body, and try to find the light of another person down here. Nothing.

Oh no.

I scramble back up the stairs.

Can I have been totally wrong? Am I crazy? Is Dubrovnik innocent?

I stop, go back down the stairs, my heart doing backflips in my chest. My own breathing is deafening in my ears.

"Please! Answer me! Are you here?"

Nothing.

I move to the boxes in the corner. I throw them aside, breaking the dishes or glasses stored in them. I strip the shelves, throwing the pickled fruits and vegetables onto the concrete. Each one detonates with a low, liquid crash.

Behind the shelves there's nothing.

Panic rises in my chest, and I feel like at any moment the world will end.

I'm whirling around when I see the extension cord. It's orange and snakes from the single bulb, down the wall and underneath the stairs.

I follow it, tracking the cord with my eyes. A large chest lurks there in the shadow of the open stairs. I yank the chest away. The floor sounds funny and hollow.

Oh, thank you.

I throw open the trapdoor and see a rough clay and stone stairway. Dubrovnik made this with his own two hands.

At the bottom is a door with a combination lock.

Racing back up the stairs, into the dark hall, I find Dubrovnik still unconscious.

"Jack! Jack! I need your help! Bring water."

No response.

He must have gotten a serious whack from Dubrovnik.

Probably has a concussion. I dash down the hall, into the kitchen. Jack's slumped over, resting his head on the counter like a bored student in class. Rummaging through the cabinets, I find a large pot, jam it underneath the faucet, and fill it with water.

I dump it all on Jack's head. Spluttering, he jerks his body upright. Blood streams down his cheek and neck.

"Stay with me, Jack. Stay awake."

He blinks. Nods once, tersely.

I fill the pot again and carry it back down the hall to where Dubrovnik lies. Did I see his hands move?

I kick him—as viciously as I can—in the stomach. He twists, and I dump the water on his face.

Dubrovnik gasps. I really did a number on his throat, I think.

"I know you're awake, you freak. Look at me."

Getting in his head is harder this time. My agitation may be to blame, or it might be his pain and discomfort from being hog-tied. I don't know. This ain't a science, I'm coming to understand.

"Look at me!"

He turns his head and opens one yellowed eye. I'm happy to report the other is swollen shut.

He's fighting me, on the inside. He knows I'm in his head.

"What's the combination?"

"Huh . . ." He voice rasps like sandpaper. "I don't know what you're talking—"

Just hearing him lie makes me furious again. So I go ahead and kick him in the stomach once more. I wish I was wearing boots. Tennis shoes aren't the best for interrogation.

"What's the combination?"

He smiles a bloody smile, the evil bastard. He's still fighting me. But just by my asking, he's thought of it. I guess he can't help but think of the answer.

12-26-05.

"Where are your car keys?"

He shakes his head, but I get a clear image of them in a drawer in the kitchen.

"Thank you for your cooperation."

He's not smiling anymore.

I dash back into the basement, down the steps, and get the lock open on my second try.

I push open the door.

He keeps her in the dark. I can hear her whimper and cringe as the door squeaks open.

■ ■ ■

We're born into pain, our constant companion through life. There are things you see, things you experience that you can never wash away or rid yourself of—*never*. They're like ink impregnated into skin, tattooed on your consciousness, malformed and dark and hideous.

There are things we see that we will never be able to unsee. They change us to the core.

What I see now in the pit, I will never speak of it, not

the way Dubrovnik kept that child, not the evidence of the things he did to her.

Never.

She huddles in the corner of the cell. In the cold.

Looking at the girl, I fall to my knees on the rough-hewn packed-clay floor. When the heaves stop, my breath coming in dim white plumes from my mouth, I can see again through my tears. I force myself to stand, force myself to go behind *her* eyes, truly terrified of what I'll find there. I see things, things he's done to her—

I'll never speak of them. *Never.*

It's as though she's always been here. She has no recollection of light, or love, or her mother's touch, or even warmth. This disgusting little hole in the ground is her world.

Her mind is a jumble, and I get strange flashes of Dubrovnik's loathsome face, sometimes sad, sometimes angry. Sometimes it is wreathed in long hair and makeup, as if he'd dressed himself as a—

Inside her pain I can barely function, I'm filled with such hatred and disgust and rage.

There's nothing I can do to help. Only time and love can heal her. All I can do is help her body.

I have to get her under covers before I can take her out of the cell. I have to cover her. I remember seeing some blankets in a box in the basement, and I dash back up the stairs and root around until I find one. Then I go back down. It nearly breaks my heart when I wrap her in the blanket and she sighs. When she rediscovers what it means to be warm again instead, my heart loosens in my chest. For a moment, I feel her remember what it's like to be human.

She's light as a doll stuffed with sawdust. I carry her into the basement and up the stairs. She's trying hard to cover her eyes.

EIGHTEEN

In the hallway I have a moment of confusion. Dubrovnik remains on the floor, squirming. But at the end of the hall he stands, silhouetted by the kitchen light. In a dress. Holding a large knife.

"Step away from him."

It's a woman's voice.

His twin. The girl's memories were of two different people. Two monsters living in the same house. Not Dubrovnik wearing a wig and makeup at all. Twins.

"No." I grip the girl tighter and she moans, maybe terrified of the pressure. Maybe of the sound of the woman's voice. I don't know. I put my foot on Dubrovnik's throat. He stops squirming. "I can crush his windpipe before you can reach me."

Where is Jack? Was that what he was trying to say, when he wanted to know . . .

She walks toward me, taking careful steps. I scrabble to try and get inside her head. Her mind is smooth and hard. She's the strong one in the relationship.

I put some pressure on Dubrovnik's neck. She stops.

"You are one ugly lady, lady."

I see her tense. Then she launches herself at me like a sprinter.

Poor child, I have to drop you to save you. The girl's body hits the floor with a dull thud, and I raise my arms to keep the knife away from my throat. It flickers at me in the low light of the hallway. The woman is on me now, and I feel a burning warmth down the length of my arm. But I'm moving forward, and her ugly face shows some surprise as I push her backward, away from Dubrovnik and the girl.

I thought I was tough. I did. I thought that when attacked, I'd be able to swing punches or gouge eyes. But when a crazy woman has a knife, fighting is gone. There are no punches, just her lurching around, trying to jam the blade inside me and me trying to embrace her, to bite her face, to stay so close to her she can't stab me.

I thrash my head to headbutt her. I writhe and kick. I try to plant a knee in her stomach or crotch. But she's as strong as Dubrovnik and faster than a cobra. I sling my arm at her to slam her nose with my elbow. Blood splatters her face, and I see a flap of skin on my forearm flopping around. I've been cut to the bone, but I don't feel anything. My hand isn't working properly anymore, but that's okay because she's blinded with a face-full of my blood.

I'm still inside the reach of her arms, and we embrace like vicious lovers. She rakes the knife down my back, still trying to stab me, but I'm moving too much for her to draw the point inward. I shove and jerk her around until I'm able to slam her against the wall. Once, twice. I outweigh her, but she's strong in the way only crazy people are strong.

I twist and shove, my fists gripping her hair and her dress, my back burning like someone ran a hot coal from my shoulder blade to my ass. I slam her head against the wood paneling, and her long hair swings into my face and sticks to the blood.

She stops wriggling for an instant, and I bring my left fist up and swing at her face. As I do, the knife glints red, and she's got it stuck in my side, buried deep.

I have five inches of steel stabbed inside me, and each inch, each millimeter, contains a mile of pain. The hurt is sharp and ever-expanding. I'll finally be released from this flesh to do the Ghost Dance, to fly like Jack in the wide blue yonder. To die. To go on permanent vacation from this meatsuit.

I can see her face, her eyes wide and excited with my bloodshed and my pain.

I'm having trouble breathing. She must have gotten a lung, because it feels like an elephant is sitting on my chest and I'm standing up, for chrissakes. But not for long. I slide down to the floor.

"Stop!" Jack. His voice is bright and angry, confident. "The police are on their way."

She slowly turns her head. She's inhumanly cold.

When she yanks the knife out, it hurts all over again. I feel pain I could only make you understand if I invaded your mind. But there's a release when the blade finally leaves my flesh. And then a looseness, as if my insides are making their exit. That's what it feels like, anyway. I don't have the energy for self-examination.

I'm still alive enough to see Jack standing at the far end of the hall, a portable phone in his hand.

"Drop the knife. They'll be here any minute."

She didn't drop the knife when I told her I was going to crush her brother's windpipe. I doubt she'll drop it now.

I don't have the air to tell Jack that, though.

He looks at me over the bodies of Dubrovnik and the girl.

"Shreve, get ready," he says, and he drops the phone. It clatters to the floor. His posture goes beyond the Angry Kid statue. For a moment I can see the man he'll become—tall, broad-shouldered, and unafraid. I'm so proud of him then that I almost forget what he's saying.

The girl. I have to cover her.

"I'm warning you. You try to hurt anyone else, and you'll regret it."

The woman is still holding the knife out to the side. In the stillness of the hallway, I can hear the *pat, pat* of the blood drops as they hit the hardwood floor.

I crawl toward the girl, using my elbows and legs. I feel like my intestines have spooled out of my stomach. I can only breathe in shallow gasps, and the taste of blood is in my mouth, unmistakable and savage.

Jack raises his hands. He shows the woman his fingers. All of them.

I reach the girl and pull myself over her, gasping apologies for lying on top of her. I do it to save her.

"Now, Shreve!"

I hear the woman's thundering footsteps, fast and urgent.

I cover my head and grip the girl tightly as the world explodes into darkness.

■ ■ ■

I remember this show, the one with the hospital and the lights and the blurry faces. Not the most original story, but not too bad either. The actors are energetic, and the dialogue is realistic. There are long moments of silence, though, and that makes me wonder if it might be a documentary. The documentaries always do the trick with the bright light and the worried voice-over of paramedics and cops. This show is no different.

"He's bleeding heavily from his side and arm. We'll need a transfusion. And he's got a punctured lung. She might have nicked his spleen, and she definitely got some of his intestines."

"The girl?"

"We found her under him. She's near-catatonic but in no danger physically."

"What caused the explosion?"

"The police officer said it looked like a grenade went off, but there's no scorch marks or fire. Just the man and woman, and the two kids."

"Looks like this one's a hero."

"Let's hope he lives to hear it."

This is the part where the light grows brighter and brighter until it whites out the frame.

And there it goes.

NINETEEN

There's a war going on, every day. You just might not know it's there.

The void left by Oprah's departure from daytime TV has really upset the balance of power. Dr. Phil vies with Dr. Dharmesh; Christy Williams grapples with the other black woman with gigantic breasts and a beautiful smile. There's a model (breasts not as big, but nice anyway) and a politician from some far northern state, all shooting for Oprah's still-warm seat.

"Hey, shooter, let's check out CNN and see what they're saying about you today."

Jerry's seventy if he's a day. Jerome Abraham Aaronson, Korean vet, teller of tall tales, sufferer of massive gallstones, and totally impenetrable to any kind of mind-tinkering or intrusion. He's a jolly iron man.

"Eh."

My side gives me a twinge of pain, but it's much better today. Dr. Stevens told me I need to move around so the tissues can get micro-tears that will help the healing process along. I read his mind when he was saying it. He didn't know if what he said was true, but it was possible and it sounded good. Dr. Stevens is in free fall. He's so terrified he'll make a mistake and someone will die that, when he leaves for lunch and sits in his car, he cries. I mean, blubbering, big-time. Titty-baby stuff. It's sad, but there's nothing I can do for him.

I stand and move to the window.

"Not that interested, Jerry."

"Let me ask you something."

"Do we have to?"

"Whoa. Mr. Big Shot. Can a person ask him a question? Is everything so bad? You can save a little girl, but you can't answer one old man's question?"

It's like he's my grandfather or something. Always with the questions.

"Okay, Jerry. Shoot."

He looks like Mel Brooks, Jerry does. When I told him that, he said, "I wish that were true and the wife looked like Anne Bancroft. Now that was one gorgeous lady."

Today he asks, "How did you know Dubrovnik had the girl in his basement?"

I sigh. Same old question. Reporters, police, all asking the same things. How did you get from Arkansas to North Carolina? How did you know he kept her in his basement?

To reporters I always respond with silence. I'm fifteen. A minor. They've got to keep their distance. At least for now.

To Jerry I tell the truth.

"I read his mind."

Jerry laughs. "No, really. How'd you know?"

"I pulled the thought right out of his head."

"Okay, you don't want to tell me. Why don't you just say so?"

I look out the window. I saw him yesterday.

He was standing on top of the UNC's main hospital building, peering at the building I'm in. He looked gaunt. Haggard. The wind whipped at his coat and tore at his hair. For a moment I was struck by the sight: a dark figure on an empty, wind-whipped roof, staring intensely.

The roof is the same height as this room, an easy view. I hobbled over to the window and banged on it, but he didn't see me. He's out there. He must really know how to jump now, because if he didn't he'd be as flat as a pancake and leaking fluids everywhere.

It's winter, and while there hasn't been any snow yet, Jack's got to be cold and hungry.

When Jack and I first came here, we each had three or four hundred dollars in our wallets. Except Jack paid for our tickets back to Jacksonville the night we discovered Dubrovnik. So he had far less. I can't remember if I gave Jack the rest of my cash or the paramedic took it off me for safekeeping. I guess I could ask the policeman standing at the door, but he's large and wide, and quite the low-watt bulb. Believe me, I've been inside his head. It's like a huge ballroom with nobody dancing in there. He reminds me a little of Ox, though I never had the pleasure of peeking inside Ox's head.

I'm back to being a ward of the state. Only it's North Carolina now, instead of Arkansas.

Jerome flips the channel to CNN. At the moment the pundits are talking about the new terrorist bombing in Pakistan and not about poor Elissa Jameson, the girl Dubrovnik kept in the cellar. Or me. Whenever I think about her, I have to believe it was all worth it. Whenever I think about myself, I have to hope it is.

There's blood in the water, and I don't just mean in daytime TV.

Quincrux is out there. I've felt the vibrations from his passing, seen his image and heard his voice in the minds of the nurses and doctors. I have no guests, though before long a lawyer or a representative from the Arkansas Department of Corrections is bound to show up. Maybe that is what's keeping Quincrux away.

He's going to be coming for me, and there's nothing I can do about it.

"You and that window. You waiting for the sky to fall?" Jerry takes a sip of water from a paper cup, grimaces, scratches his ass through the itchy hospital gown. "How 'bout a game of Double Shutter?"

Anything to stop his questions.

Jerry tells me Double Shutter is an ancient game invented by his ancestors. But it looks like it was packaged by Hasbro. Domino-like pieces are lodged on small axles inside a red metal tin, so you can flip down the numbers. Two rows, one to ten, going left to right and then back again on the rear row. You roll the dice; then you turn down the corresponding tiles or a combination of tiles that equals the sum. It's harder than it looks. Lowest score wins.

I walk over to Jerry. My side does hurt, but far less than a week ago. Maybe Dr. Stevens was right about the micro-tears. I should tell him. Might make him feel better.

My arm and fingers are still numb. I had to crap in a bag for nearly two weeks, and they removed a foot or two of my intestines—which is a nice conversation piece, I guess. When I look at myself shirtless in the mirror, I can count my ribs and see the bones of my pelvis. There's the puckered forget-me-not gunshot wound that Billy Cather gave me, so long ago, gracing my right shoulder and balanced now by cottonfields of dressing gauzing my left side, courtesy of the Dubrovnik twins. My left forearm is pink and shiny with new skin from where Matilda tried to skin me.

Pretty worthless to look at, really, this meatsuit. I could shuck it off and fly into the wild blue yonder and never return. What would that be like? Weightlessness? The cold empty spaces between the stars? A warm bath? Nothing?

I look at the gunshot wound. Old now, with no pain except for that in my heart.

I ran away once before and lost my little dude, my Vig. I have this wound as a reminder. I can't run again. Sometimes I feel like my insides might spill out of me, onto the floor. It's happened before. So I remain where I am, looking at my scars. My reminders. They're a symbol. A tether. A cage.

I'll stay incarcerado.

Back when I was dealing, I was thicker, to say the least. But I wouldn't recommend the Knife in Your Guts Diet Plan.

Matilda Dubrovnik did a number on me. She cut me deep and removed the possibility I'll ever be a classical pianist. Or a mountain climber.

Jerry and I play a quick game of Double Shutter, me standing by his bed while he holds the game on his blanket. They operated on Jerry to remove gallstones. They could have just let him pass them, but the pain from passing them might have screwed with his heart condition. Or they could have just operated to put more money in their pockets.

I score fifteen, a seven and an eight remaining, which isn't too bad. On Jerry's turn he shuts it down, closing all the tiles. The old bastard. He does that every time nearly. It's uncanny.

"Why do you even play me? You never lose."

"I'm waiting for the magic to happen." He winks. He might irritate me, but I can't stay permanently ticked. Well, maybe at night. He snores something fierce.

Nurse Larsson comes in, checks Jerry's chart, and then tells him he's off for another test. She helps him into a wheelchair.

On their way out, Jerry asks the nurse to stop. He turns his head toward me.

"Don't do anything stupid while I'm gone, okay? Like go running off to be another hero?"

"I'm not a hero. Why do you keep saying that?"

He smiles. "Be good, Shreve."

Jerry's a good dude. I feel sorry that he's peeing rocks.

"I'll try, boss."

Nurse Larsson wheels him out just as the announcer on CNN starts to talk about Elissa Jameson.

"And now for developing news on the horrific Elissa Jameson story. Forensics has identified the remains of two other children on the property, meaning the Dubrovnik twins held captive other children. Now we have forensic anthropologist Dr. Cherri Pittle to talk to us a little about what the police on the scene might have found . . ."

The Dubrovniks, the house, the girl—it all seems like someone else's memory.

Last week I was watching the news, and my face popped up on-screen. And then an exterior shot of good old Casimir, and then a driver's license mug shot of Moms.

So they discovered I'm a fugitive. But no word on Jack. Which makes me think someone is covering up his existence. And that someone has to be Quincrux.

Today, the anchor and the doctor consultant drone on about the case, and I return to staring out the window and letting the noise wash over me.

I watch for Jack. This time I'll be ready.

I hear someone come in, and I turn. An orderly. But he's staring at me intently, and he's without a mop or a cart. He walks over to the guest chair and sits down. He's got a pronounced limp.

He crosses his legs slowly, very slowly, never breaking eye contact. He looks infinitely bored with the situation. He puts his hands in his lap in a delicate manner, making me think of Englishmen on AMC.

Maybe he's a reporter. Why didn't the guard stop him?

For a long while he stares at me.

"What do you want?" I ask. "The trash is over there." I point to the bin under the sink.

"So, Mr. Cannon, it seems you have proved more resourceful than either Ilsa or I guessed. How long have you hidden your skills?"

Ah.

Quincrux. He's possessing this guy. Driving him like a remote-controlled car. He must be near. In the building.

I don't feel so good.

They say honesty is the best policy, but I think they're idiots. I don't have any problem allowing Quincrux to go on believing something that's not true. He doesn't realize that he gave me this ability. So I stay quiet.

"No matter. No matter, Mr. Cannon. I can't take you out of here now, not with," he tosses his head in the direction of the dull-witted police officer, "that gentleman and the reporters swarming the lobby and the atrium. But rest assured, I will take you."

That doesn't sound so good. Might as well go on offense. Nothing to lose except everything.

"How's the leg?"

His face darkens. I do believe I've found a sore spot with Mr. Quincrux.

"Ah. Quite a surprise Mr. Graves gave us, I must admit. The doctors tell me I'll require years of painful physical therapy if I ever want to walk without a limp."

"Nice." I can't help but feel smug. "And the witch?"

"The witch?" He looks puzzled for a moment, and then he smiles. "Is that what you call her? How appropriate. Unfortunately, her body did not survive. Her spine was totally severed. Multiple internal injuries and brain damage. She barely had enough time to extract herself and occupy a new host. I fear she's not much use to me now, unless she receives more hearty sustenance."

His eyes never leave me. I don't like the way he says that: *sustenance.*

"What about Norman?"

"Norman?"

"Yeah. The guy who was with you when we blew up in your face." I try not to let the stress sound in my voice. "Did he make it?"

"I must not have made myself clear. Ilsa needed a new host. She took the vessel nearest and easiest to inhabit. Maybe we should start referring to her as 'him' now."

I step toward him, bringing up my fists. I have the barely contained urge to punch his self-satisfied face.

He raises his eyebrows and inclines his head slightly in an innocent, oh-I'm-sorry-did-I-offend-you? kind of way.

He can talk and talk and be polite as Jeeves, but he's a brute. A monster.

"Taking a new host is . . ." He shrugs. "It is hard. On everyone concerned. It takes a while to integrate."

"You mean take over." I spit at his feet. "Rape."

"Semantics." He brushes an invisible speck of lint off his dirty orderly uniform. He's a sandy-headed man, slim build, mid-fifties. Three days' beard. Wedding ring. I wonder whether he's watching this from somewhere or if Quincrux has tamped him down beyond awareness.

This is not good. This is so not good. How long do these freaks live? The witch took someone else's body?

"We live long. But not forever."

Maybe the surprise shows on my face. Quincrux chuckles.

"No, I did not read your mind, dear boy. The day is coming soon when you will have to try and keep me out, if you can. However, I do not need to read your mind to know what you are thinking. I can make quite adroit guesses on my own."

"What do you want?"

"I want to come to an arrangement with you."

"You killed a man. The biker—"

He remains silent, implacable. Then he bows his head once, slowly bringing it toward his chest and then back, his gaze never leaving me.

"I have killed. Yes, this is true."

More than one. Many, even.

I don't want to hear this. I do not want to hear it.

He goes on.

"I believe you are in contact with Mr. Graves. If you turn him over to me, I will make sure you do not end up on Ilsa's . . . er . . . should I say, Norman's . . . menu." He smiles. "I can further guarantee that we will protect you. Give you employment. Teach you how to use your powers."

"Who's we?"

"A very old society."

"Like a government agency?"

"Related. Closely related."

"What does that mean?"

Quincrux clears his throat. "Never you mind. All questions will be answered if and when Mr. Graves is turned over."

"What will you do to him? Give him to the witch?"

"Hardly. He is a soldier. He will be used."

"And what am I?"

"That is what we are trying to determine." He stands and dusts off his overall pants legs as if he were wearing a suit. "You are, if you will pardon the pun, a loose cannon. Unquantifiable. But once we have our . . . match, our bit of mental contention, if you will . . . I'll know exactly your final . . . eh . . . disposition."

This guy. Coming here. To threaten. To deal. For Jack.

Suddenly I'm furious, more furious than I ever thought I could be. I feel like burning embers have been placed in my chest, on my tongue.

I won't let him. I'll kick his ass out.

"No." I hit him with everything I've got. A full mental barrage. "No deal."

He sticks for a moment, but I rip at him, at the invisible tissues, the mental barbs and defenses. And he gives way before me. He gives way to my wrath.

I feel Biblical, casting out devils. I don't know. I feel beyond myself.

But I get a twinge that Quincrux is laughing, that he's amused. He knew I'd do it. And he let me. He goaded me into it.

The orderly shudders, blinks, and then looks like he's going to fall. I step forward, grab his arm, and ease him back into the guest chair.

"Where am I?" he says in a voice that's hopeless and utterly lost.

TWENTY

Life in the hospital is far worse than life at Casimir.

The food sucks. I mean, how can you mess up pudding? Or popsicles?

The empty-headed police officer infuriates me. He won't let me out of this room. I could force him, get inside that gigantic echoing cranium and pull some levers, but . . . I'd rather not. I'll have to do it eventually, to somebody. But I can't bolt until I make contact with Jack.

The nurses bug. Seriously. You can hear their thighs rubbing when they walk around in their squishy, lumbar-supporting shoes. They're always checking bandages or removing stitches. Sticking needles in my ass.

They released Jerry this morning. They forced him into a wheelchair and trucked him out, but not before he grabbed my hand.

"Shreve, you'll be a good boy, won't you?"

"Sure."

"They can't keep you in here forever. Someone will be here to get you soon, I'm sure. It won't be long now."

Understatement of the year. I think he meant it in a different way than it sounded to me.

I nodded.

"So, here." He pressed something in my hand. A business card. It read *Jerry Aaronson*, *Asset Consulting*, with a phone number, e-mail, and website.

"What's asset consulting?"

"Eh. Just like it sounds. But don't worry about that." He covered my hand with both of his. "If you ever need anything. Anything. You'll give me a call, right?"

"Sure. Can you take me with you?"

He laughed. You can see gold fillings and bridgework in the back of his mouth when he laughs. He's got a big laugh. To match his heart, I guess.

"If only I could. I need someone to beat at Double Shutter." At that, Nurse Larsson cleared her throat, indicating it was time for him to leave. "Be good."

I can't trust anyone. And I'm alone. No Jack, no Vig. No Coco. Not even Booth or Moms. I've always had someone to look after, or someone to rebel against. I don't know what to do with myself.

So now I'm back to watching the window.

On the inside, back in Casimir, you're never alone. There's always someone near, some kid pestering you, some bull eying you, your cellmate snoring—or going explodey, or getting interrogated by mind-jumping lunatics.

In the hospital there's even more noise and more commotion. But somehow it seems emptier. Lonelier.

That might have to do with all the antiseptics.

I'm not much for waiting. For watching.

But I don't have long.

■■■

I'm counting the birds and clouds when he lands on the opposite roof and starts looking around. He's got on a new jacket, puffier than the last, and a knit woolen hat pulled down around his ears. It looks cold out there.

I'm ready for him.

The nurses were kind enough to provide me with paper and markers during my convalescence. You know, because I'm just a poor little kid and of course I'd want to doodle and maybe turn over the drawings to the state-appointed head-shrinker. I dash to my bedside table, grab some of the paper, and write a big Q in black ink on one page. At the window, I slap it against the glass, Q facing out, and wait.

After a moment, Jack waves.

I write on another sheet IS HERE. Big capital letters.

Jack nods and points down.

I write YES and slap it on the window.

He makes the OK sign and then pantomimes riding a horse. No, not a horse. A broom.

I write NOT HERE. Then on another sheet, SHE LIVED.

I guess I've just discovered what newsmen and politicians have known for decades: lying is easier in print.

NORMAN DID TOO.

It's hard to tell across the thirty or forty yards that separate us, but I think Jack looks relieved.

He holds up his hands and makes a gesture. He's too far away for me to make it out.

WHAT?

He points to me, then himself, then fake runs.

YES. HOW?

He points up. At the roof of my building.

Oh. I don't know if I'm ready for this, but the point is irrelevant since I hear someone behind me clear her throat.

"Shreve? What are you doing?"

It's Nurse Larsson. For once her thighs remained quiet. Perfect timing for them to hush their whisking.

"Uh. Nothing." I scoop up all the papers and crumple them up. "Just doodling."

Behind Larsson stands the state shrink, come to talk, again. Helen Kristeva. She's good-looking, but she doesn't wear any makeup and she asks more questions than Jerome Aaronson.

She steps forward and says, "May I see?"

I ball up the paper, tight.

"Just doodling."

"I'd like to see."

"Maybe later." You can't say no to these people. You have to make small compromises so their radar doesn't go up.

She smiles. It's a patient, I'm-here-to-listen smile. She pads over—wool socks with sandals—and plants herself in the guest chair where Quincrux questioned me.

This could be him. I have to check.

Entering her head is as painless as entering the bathroom and almost as clean. In this hospital, that's saying something.

Is it weird that someone who wants to get into my skull is so easy to penetrate?

"Let me guess. You've never been to Maryland?"

She looks puzzled. "No. Now that you mention it, I haven't. Is it nice?"

"No clue. I haven't been there either."

She pulls out a notepad and scribbles something on it. Through her eyes I read what she wrote: *Conversation—Defense tactics.*

"It's not defense tactics."

She looks surprised, cranes her head to peer behind her, checking for a mirror.

"So, how are you doing, Shreve?"

"Fine."

"Fine?"

"Yeah." No reason to lie here. She's as clear as a glass of water. "Maybe a little bored."

"I'd think you'd want your life a little calmer. You've been on your own for what? Three months now?"

"On my own? More like fifteen years. Or do you mean escaped?"

"Okay. Escaped, then. It must be a relief to be somewhere safe and secure."

I'm about to ask her where that is but stop myself.

She scribbles *Paranoia* on her pad.

Am I that shifty? Is everything out there for display on my face?

I need to get back on script. I need to answer the way she expects me to answer. So she'll go away.

I'm itching to turn and look out the window, to see if Jack's still there. But if I do, she might see him. Or Larsson might see him while she's stripping the sheets on my bed. Anything they see here, Quincrux will pluck from their heads, as sure as sin.

"So, how are your wounds? Do they pain you?"

"My side hurts a little. I'm still numb in my hand."

"You'll be starting physical therapy soon."

"Yeah. That's what they tell me."

Underneath *Paranoia*, she writes *Extremely wary—understandable—history of abuse.*

Jesus. This woman. I should make her stand up and dance a jig or something. Maybe start talking only in gibberish and have a seizure so she can get a taste of her own medicine.

Ah.

I can't do that.

Damn.

"You don't seem to want to talk about your wounds. Is the memory too painful?"

"What memory?"

"The Dubrovniks' house? When they wounded you."

"No. That memory isn't painful at all. The girl is safe now, and the woman got what she deserved. And he'll get what he deserves soon."

"Surely you must still have strong emotions regarding their capture of you."

"They didn't capture me. I told this to the police. We . . ." Ooops. Almost let it slip. "I went there to save the girl. I broke in."

More notes: *Persists in delusion.*

"Where did you get your degree, lady? I am not persisting in my delusion. What exactly do you think happened there?"

"What I think isn't the point of this conversation."

Responds to memory of incidence with aggression.

I throw up my hands. Either they're trying to keep me here, or they're trying to get me out of here as fast as possible and into the psych ward. I'm not an idiot. I read books. I watch the Discovery Channel. No one keeps a kid without health insurance in the hospital for this long unless there's something to gain. But what's being gained, I don't think I'll ever know. I don't even have the energy to dig around in her skull to find out.

Something's going on behind the scenes. And the fact that my face is on CNN every fifteen minutes isn't helping. Lucky for me, I'll be gone before it all plays out.

I shouldn't do it. I really shouldn't do it. But I do. I make her add a little something at the bottom of her notebook page.

I am a stupid cow.

She's not. But damn, she sure doesn't listen for a shrink.

TWENTY-ONE

By the time Larsson and Kristeva leave, it's night and I can't see if Jack's out there anymore. I have to assume he's squatting in the hospital complex, probably on a roof, but I'll have to wait before I know for sure.

The orderly brings a tray with stuff that looks like food but doesn't taste like it. I leave it on the rolling table, untouched.

I'm lying in bed when the meaty officer goes on break and is replaced by the skinny, weasel-faced policeman. He comes into the room, makes sure I'm here.

"Hey, sport. How ya feeling?"

"Fine. When are they sending me back to Arkansas?"

"No idea, kid. The news says you might stay here."

"In the hospital?"

"Nah. North Carolina."

"Why?"

"Trial."

Like hell. I'll never get to the trial. Quincrux will stop me before I have a chance. Spirit me away or wipe my brain.

All signs point to get-the-hell-outta-here.

I let the weasel get his coffee and read the paper, kick back in his chair in front of my door. I'll let him have his nap and chat with the nurse whose thighs don't whisk. She's got nice legs for a nurse. I can give him that much at least. Because, after I use him, he probably won't be trusted to be a policeman anymore.

It sucks, but that's the way it's got to be.

▪▪▪

The sun hasn't come up yet. It's lighter in the east, above the winking, electric glow of the hospital complex. There's a forest of buildings out there, and Jack could be watching from the roof of any of them.

A nurse comes in to peek on me, and I have to take her over. I have to, if I want to escape. To survive. I don't have time to pick and choose.

It's not an easy thing, possessing a person. I don't mean simply skimming the surface, reading her thoughts. I mean really getting in there and using her body, looking through her eyes, speaking with her mouth. Walking. Turning doorknobs. Even the simplest action produces so much sensory input, it's hard to retain control. Sometimes I find it hard to believe Quincrux could ever have controlled the whole yard at Casimir, but other times . . . That's like—I don't know—godlike power if he can do it. The witch's number of five seems more realistic, though still a bit out there. I'm so new to all of this. Maybe the trick is to enjoy it.

And what if one of the people were from Maryland?

But more than my unease at possessing people, I don't like that while you're in there, they have to go. You have to boot them out into the wide blue yonder. What does that leave them open to?

I'm not really comfortable doing that to this nurse. She's just doing her job. She came to work tonight never expecting to have someone go all Exorcist on her.

But I have to see Vig again. I have to see Coco. Even Moms and Booth.

I don't want my life to end here. Snuffed out by Quincrux because I won't give him what he wants—because I won't give him Jack.

I dig around in her head until I know what I need to know. I turn her around and march her out to the break room down the hall. I have her take from her locker an extra set of the green pajamas all the hospital staff wear. I'd rather they be a man's size, but I'll take what I can get. Anything is better than trying to escape with my butt hanging out.

From her wallet she removes her cash: forty-six dollars. No one carries around cash these days. Then she checks other lockers until she finds one that isn't locked. Inside are a blue-jean jacket and a pair of tennis shoes.

As she's walking back to my room, I'm struck by a moment of dizziness and have to put out my arms. Possession is like having two TV shows on at once and trying to follow both stories. Your consciousness is always tugging at you to reenter your own body, but you're also getting input from your . . .

Your host. That's what Quincrux called it. Your vessel.

God, I'm everything my mother said I am. And worse. So much worse.

I'm the devil now.

The nurse brings me the clothes, the shoes, and the money—nodding and smiling at Weasel on the way into my room—and lays it all down on my bed. Weasel never suspects.

I walk her out of the room, down the hall, past the nurses' station.

"Hey! Lacy? Where are you going? We need you to check on Mrs. Peterson in thirteen. Lacy?"

It's like moving a boulder, but I make her turn her head and say, "Okay. Be right back."

It sounds a little mushy-mouthed, to be honest. But I don't have a lot of practice at this.

"Are you okay? Lacy?"

Walking is easier than talking. I get her legs working again and move her over to the elevators. Raise arm, press down arrow.

"I'm fine." That sounded better. Less mushy-mouthed. For a moment I'm amazed by the feel of my tongue forming the words. Her tongue. It's hard to keep our bodies straight.

The two night nurses stare at me, and I stare back.

"Just gotta check something." That bit actually sounds good.

The doors slide open, and I move inside. The line between puppet and puppeteer has disappeared now. Once I'm sure the elevator is heading down, I let her go. I have to. I could get trapped in here.

This is the worst part, really. Once you take hold of someone, the body doesn't want to let you go. But Lacy is out there, hammering to get back in. And now that I'm thinking in her body, using her brain, referring to myself as I while wearing her skin, my . . . awareness . . . my soul, even . . . doesn't want to leave her.

I'm descending, rocking back and forth in the elevator carriage and watching the numbers decrease over the door. On the inside, incarcerado, it's a fight to unclench. To let go.

That bit of me that is purely me twists and frets to be let loose. And Lacy screams to be let back in. She hammers at me, she writhes and squirms.

Suddenly I'm out and gasping back in my room.

"Thank you. I'm so sorry."

Nothing. She's gone. I only have a few moments until she puts everything together. God, I hope I haven't infected her with this . . . horror. This terrible gift.

No more time for remorse. Only time for rock and roll.

The Weasel is even harder to possess. Has he been to Maryland? To someplace nearby? Does that matter? Do the witch and Quincrux have the same problems with Marylanders as I do? Or can they overcome it, the mysterious rider?

Weasel's older, for one, and his grip on his body is more tenacious, maybe. I have to force myself in, bully my way through. And the Weasel is strong. It's a fight. He doesn't understand what's happening, but he instinctively knows he doesn't want it to continue. He throws up defenses. His body tightens, and he bites his tongue, hard, until blood comes and the pain blossoms, bright and overwhelming, and I lose ground. I feel my control slip. I'm sliding back to my body.

But the pain dies, and I have real reason to fear that this is my only way out. So I have to get rough. MeShreve closes his eyes, and I tear myself away from my birthbody. I hurl myself through the darkness between lights, and I invade Weasel. On all fronts, I attack. I fill his senses, his eyes, his skin. He can hear and taste me. I fill his mind with me, my essence, that part of me that is nothing but me—not body, not habit, not blood or flesh, but me. Solely. And I hurt him. While he fights me, I race through the chambers of his mind. I find his moments of weakness. His hurts and betrayals. His failures and losses. All of it, I force on him. I make him relive it.

He flees into the beyond. And I have control.

We stand. MeWeasel remains outside the door, and MeShreve walks out, clad in the new clothes that are tight in the legs and crotch. The shoes are too large, making walking more difficult.

But once those parts of me near each other—MeShreve and MeWeasel both outside my room—we/I turn and walk toward the stairwell down the hall. Feet match time. Arms swing as one.

"Hey! He's not allowed out of his room."

Nurse Larsson stands down the hall, by the nurses' station.

"Hey! Jimmy! He's not allowed . . ."

I turn my heads and look back. She's still, a dazed look on her face. She shudders. And then she smiles.

Walking forward, she limps.

"Where are you going, Mr. Cannon?" It's strange to hear Quincrux's inflections coming from Larsson's mouth. Her voice is high, so squeaky. I thought that was affected. I guess not.

But she doesn't sound bored. Quincrux has finally invested himself in something—catching me. But he isn't assaulting me mentally. So, what does that mean?

Now is not the time to chat with Quincrux. Now's the time to haul ass.

It's hard to get both parts of me to move in unison, but once I do, I clear the twenty yards to the stairwell fast and come to an abrupt stop. MeWeasel yanks open the door, steps through. MeShreve follows after.

I take the steps two at a time. Two flights up I have a moment of vertigo and feel a hitch in MeShreve's side. The sutures have been removed for a week, but I'm still sore and it feels like something might have ripped in there.

We keep climbing up the stairwell. At the top, the door is locked.

A sign proclaims, ROOF ACCESS FORBIDDEN. The phrase is repeated in Spanish. Thoughtful.

I shove at the push-bar release. It depresses, but the door remains unmoved.

MeShreve sits down. Leans back into the cinderblock walls. Closes his eyes. Below, the sound of feet echoes up the stairwell. Doors are opening. I transfer all my awareness into MeWeasel.

I throw myself at the door, shoulder first, once. Twice. The pain is outrageous and huge. It looks so easy on TV. I kick at the center of the door. Nothing except jarring vibrations running up and down my frame.

I'm about to throw myself against the door again when I remember.

I pull the gun from Weasel's holster. I haven't had a lot of experience with pistols, but I know most guns have a safety. I find it and flip the switch.

"Mr. Cannon!" The voice echoes up the stairwell. This is the real Quincrux speaking, not one of his drones. "This is futile. There are no exits from the roof. Either you realize this and know something I don't know—which I find highly unlikely—or I have you trapped."

What I'm about to do, they do on TV. I hope it works here. I step back from the door, point the pistol at the point where the lock looks most likely, and fire. The result is a huge noise that nearly jars me out of Weasel's body and the flash of a ricochet.

I fire again. And again.

I throw myself at the door. It hurts like the dickens. *Sorry, Weasel, you're most likely going to lose your job and be sore as hell tomorrow. But it can't be helped.*

The door and locking mechanism looks worse for wear. My ears are ringing as I bring the gun up into a firing position, take aim, and fire again. And again.

When the gun clicks, I stuff it back into the holster and kick the door. It starts to give.

I split myself into component parts and look at the close confines of the stairwell through four eyes. I can hear them coming now, closer and closer. Quincrux must have quite a few drones. Ten maybe. Twenty. All slaves of Quincrux. An assload of folks are going to lose their jobs tomorrow.

MeShreve stands next to MeWeasel, and together I throw myself at the door. Ooof. Again, two shoulders to metal.

Then I hear a bright ringing sound, and cold air rushes past me as the door swings open.

It's time to let MeWeasel go, I think. They're coming, and I don't have time to mess around being sweet. MeShreve reaches out and takes the pistol from the holster.

There's nothing like ripping part of your soul out of another person. You could say it's like ripping a bandage off a wound, but only if that wound covered both your inside and your outside, was matted with blood, and you were as hairy as a freaking bear. And you did it all in an instant.

Weasel shudders, blinks.

"I'm sorry, man." I flip the pistol around and grip it by the barrel. "I hate to do this, but it might make tomorrow go a little easier for you."

When I clock him across the top of his head with the pistol, he drops. It is the only thing that has worked out exactly like it happens on TV. Well, not exactly. They never show the guilt on TV.

After a moment of fumbling I manage to pop open one of the Batman-like containers on Weasel's belt and pull out a heavy, black metal object that I've seen on TV but have never really manipulated before. A magazine holding bullets. I turn the pistol, and there on the side of the grip is a small, round button. I jab at it, my chest working up and down like a bellows, and the clip pops from the bottom and clatters on the floor.

I can hear their treads on the stairs. Closer now, so much closer.

I peek through the open space between handrails, down the empty well of space. They're maybe two floors down, judging from the shadows. Walking slowly up like zombies, maybe. Shambling.

Limping. All of them, in unison.

After a couple of tries I manage to get the magazine inserted into the pistol and then stand there, dazed for a moment, trying to figure out what comes next. I close my eyes to remember what it looked like when action heroes handled guns on television. It seems they pull on the top of the gun or something. They point it up and pull down on the slidy thing on top.

I point the gun at the ceiling, grab the top of it, and pull downward.

The sound it makes, *snick*, sounds exactly like it does on television. I think it might be ready.

Both hands on the pistol, I lift it and point it down the stairwell.

"What was that sound, Mr. Cannon? It sounded suspiciously like you reloaded the unfortunate policeman's sidearm. Is that correct?"

I say nothing and wait, sighting the bottom of the stairwell. The first of the limpers will round the corner any second now. How many bullets do these things hold, anyway?

"We are not so different, Mr. Cannon, I should think," Quincrux says, and he chuckles. It sounds almost as if he's proud of me, glad that I fulfilled his expectations. "We are one, you and I."

For a moment, before my eyes, there's the genial, open face of the big-bellied trucker in Chattahoochee, surprise widening his expression as we ran past him out the door into the sun-hammered parking lot. I remember Jack caught in midstride, running, his hair a wild spray about him as the air turned to flying shards of glass and a haze of blood droplets suspended in the light like silt in a glass of water.

They're almost in view, Quincrux's slaves.

I straighten my arm, sighting along the barrel. It's bizarre how heavy a gun can be.

Too heavy.

I toss down the gun. It clatters and spins even as I do, wheeling around and pushing through the door.

Out the door, into the cold and wind. The sky is lightening now, pink with wispy purple tendrils like long, gnarly fingers.

They're behind me, and I run forward, looking for any way off the roof, for Jack. For a miracle.

The roof, covered in brown and grey pea gravel, crunches under my feet, and the steam from some metal ventricle drools white stuff toward the overcast sky.

"Shreve!" Jack. I turn. He's pale and emaciated. He looks ghostly. The boy hasn't been eating.

He stands a few feet away on the gravel of the roof, next to gigantic industrial air units. The roof sprouts antennae and large, dull gray metal boxes with wires running away into other metal boxes. "I heard the shots."

"It's Quincrux. He's coming now. Right behind—"

The door bangs open.

I see Larsson and Lacy, a doctor, and a young man in a hospital gown. More people move behind them.

"Move to the side, Shreve." Jack straightens his arm like pointing a pistol and spreads out his fingers. Flat out, all six.

"No. You can't, Jack. They're innocent."

His shoulders tighten as if preparing for the recoil of a gun.

"Remember Florida, Jack! The man at the hotel!" My voice is hoarse, shrill, like some unturned and ancient violin.

They stand, motionless, looking at us with the same grin spread across many faces.

"Ah, Mr. Graves. It is such a pleasure to see you again."

I shudder at the echoing effect of all the people, all the Quincrux drones, speaking as one. Blood pours from each of their noses, dripping down their chins to splatter and spread on their shirts, their dresses, their uniforms, giving them all a gory, carnivorous look.

They speak as one. It's more than just a chorus. It's as if Quincrux has swollen to unimaginable size and these drones, these zombies, they're his cult and his new flesh and his choir. That whatever evil drives him, whatever desire, surged and throbbed in his chest and then burst forth to find other people to infect. And given half a chance, it would infect the world, everybody, moving like lightning from treetop to church steeple to telephone pole, a dark electricity ready to corrupt all of existence.

I almost wish I had the gun again.

I say, "Quincrux is here. He's just a coward and lets his drones take the heat for him." I point at the door. "He's probably hiding in the stairwell."

They take a step forward. All with the same limp.

"No one needs to be hurt, Mr. Graves, if you and Mr. Cannon will just come with me quietly. I have the power to smooth this all over, to make these people forget. To make Mr. Cannon's legal troubles disappear. If only you'll come with me."

"He's lying. He's gonna feed me to the witch," I say.

Jack blinks, turns, and grabs my arm.

"This way."

He runs south. The hospital complex buildings are arrayed on a north–south arc. A neighboring building is close, very close, and I'm worried that Jack wants me to do what I think he wants me to do.

"Stop!" Quincrux's slaves chant. "We can come to an agreement!"

Jack stops right at the edge of the roof and looks back at me. "We get across, he won't be able to follow. Not with that limp."

The opposite roof is fifteen feet away, and lower.

Oh, no.

"I don't like this, Jack."

"What're you going to do, stay here?"

I hear the crunch of Quincrux's slaves coming forward.

"I cannot let you leave, I'm afraid."

Jack pulls me back ten feet from the ledge. I look toward the ruined door, and Quincrux appears in the frame, behind the group of people. He's in his dark suit and hat, but has accessorized with a cane.

"Now," Jack says, and he tugs me forward.

We run.

When I reach the lip of the abyss, I jump, gripped by Jack.

Everything seems to slow, and I feel a tremendous wrenching on my injured arm as Jack explodes into the air, dragging me with him. But, simultaneously, I feel a massive hammering inside my skull, and I don't even have a chance to conjure up a jawbreaker before Quincrux has gained a foothold in my mind.

I'm trying to fend him off as I plummet over the abyss. My arm is wrenched away from Jack. The lift from his pulse is gone, and I'm falling toward the mirrored face of the building rushing at me.

I can perceive that even Quincrux is alarmed at how fast the building's hard corner rushes at me.

When I hit the edge, I feel my side rip wide open. Even as I scramble to catch hold, it feels like the Dubrovnik woman has stabbed me all over again.

The pain has driven Quincrux out. My bandaged, numb hand slips and my legs swing downward, and suddenly I'm scratching at tar paper and gravel and brickwork as my feet dangle three hundred feet above the ground.

Jack lands lightly on the gravel of the roof and rushes toward me.

It's now that Quincrux resumes his assault. And I'm like tissue paper. He's inside my mind like he's never left. But I've learned a few things since we last met.

I take the fight to him, like I did with Marvin.

I try to possess his body.

His attention wavers, and I'm back in my head again. Which is terrifying because I'm going to fall.

Quincrux shoves all resistance aside. The jawbreaker is shattered, the windows are blown out, and I'm just an observer in the wild blue yonder. Once again. Turnabout is fair play, they say. I guess I deserve everything I get. I'm sure Lacy and the Weasel would agree.

My wounded hand slips from the edge, and I'm left hanging by one arm. I hope Quincrux does something about that.

Jack throws himself onto his stomach and grabs my wrist.

"Don't let go. I have you."

"It seems, Mr. Graves, we are at an impasse."

Quincrux's words coming from my own mouth make me feel like I've betrayed Jack. I'm a Judas to my only friend.

"You can release Mr. Cannon, and then flee. I will not be able to stop you, not with your gravity-defying abilities. Mr. Cannon will, of course, fall to his death."

Jack's brow furrows, but he doesn't need long to figure out what's going on.

"I am quite impressed with your abilities. Having reviewed the videotapes, I knew some of your power... but this! Flight! This is an exciting development."

"Shut up."

I'm still there, still seated in the flesh, even though I'm not in control. Quincrux's puppet, I swing my bad hand up and grasp Jack's other arm. Jack shifts his hold, and now both of my hands are clasping his wrists and he's gripping mine.

"I will not vacate this boy willingly, Mr. Graves. In a moment, if we cannot come to an agreement, I will make him release you and fall. Unless you give me your word, you will remain where you are. I have vessels on the way to you now." I hear a banging coming from somewhere on this roof. It looks like Quincrux's cavalry is here.

Quincrux clears my throat. "He can't hold on much longer. His wounds have reopened, and I—"

My bad hand slips out of Jack's grasp. I feel my arm stretch, and suddenly my shoulder dislocates. It pops right out of the socket like I'm a roasted chicken and someone is pulling off a wing. There's only flesh—muscle and tendon—tethering me to life. The pain is excruciating.

But when it ebbs, I realize Quincrux is out.

"Jack, let me go. You can't save me. But you can save yourself if you run now—"

"No!"

"Go. You can escape. I can't!"

He shakes his head furiously.

The assault begins again. Quincrux rips away at my pain and desperation, and with the last of my strength, I keep him out. I keep him out.

I release Jack's hands.

For an instant, I hang in the air and there's a brightness all around. I fall, tumbling downward, and above all I feel the loss of never seeing my family again. Of never playing Kick the Can with Jack in the woods where we lived for that week. Of never hugging Booth, the big idiot.

I fall. The wind rushes like a tempest in my ears, and I close my eyes for the last time. I can tumble away forever now from the things Moms said. From what Quincrux wants me to become. I'm not those things. I'm nothing now but air and rushing wind and pain. Incarcerado no longer.

A tremor. I shudder, and something passes through me.

The air wavers, my body twists. The world keels over and rights itself. Suddenly I'm rising up.

I'm rising.

I look up, and Jack stands at the edge of the roof, his hair tousled wildly by the frigid wind, his hands out, beckoning me to come to him, like he's waving me over to join his kickball team. He's got a surprised look on his face.

The boy who pushed everything away, he's drawing me in.

I rise.

When my feet touch the roof, we're facing each other. He's panting, and I can see that, even in the cold, sweat is beading on his forehead and wetting his temples.

The rooftop's pounding stops with a boom and a crash. Quincrux's slaves are on the roof now, and they're coming for us.

"Go, Jack. You can make it."

"No. We'll stick together. Look what happens when I'm not around to look after you."

I'm too tired to laugh. Blood is seeping through my

stolen hospital duds. I can't feel the fingers of my bandaged arm, and the other arm hangs useless and throbbing. I'd almost appreciate Quincrux taking over now so I wouldn't have to feel all this.

Jack comes over to me. He puts my bandaged arm over his shoulder and helps me walk toward the waiting crowd of smiling Quincruxes.

Sirens sound below us. It looks like this party is about to get even bigger. The smiles on the faces fade.

But I don't care. I don't care.

"I guess we can't call you Mr. Explodey anymore."

Jack snorts.

"Was that like a superhug you just gave me?"

"Shut up, Shreve."

Quincrux's drones surround us and lead us into the building, back down to earth.

TWENTY-TWO

On the inside, some things change and some things stay the same. I can't get inside Booth's head—he's like a steel ball, smooth and impenetrable—and I don't think I'd want to if I could. But I can still get under his skin.

But we're fairly chummy now. He doesn't lurk about, glaring at me, and I don't deal the sweet stuff or manipulate the wards. He's figured out something funny happened, but he's never had the balls to ask me outright. And he's never asked what happened to Jack.

▪▪▪

Today is Saturday, which means no class, the commissary does a booming business, and mail call and visitors are allowed—if you have anyone who cares about you enough to visit or send crackers, cookies, or cash.

The notoriety that greeted me when I returned to Casimir faded fast. It didn't hurt that I never spoke a word about what happened to anyone, not reporter, priest, or police. Since the events of last winter I've been the model citizen of Casimir Pulaski Juvenile Detention Center for Boys, home until my eighteenth birthday. Despite my hero status, they extended my term.

The board members were quite ticked off that I escaped from their institution of juvenile rehabilitation and went off and had an adventure, if you want to call it that. You read about adventures, you watch them on TV, but you never realize how hurt you'll be at the other end when an actual adventure craps you out.

So I'll be here for the next two and a half years.

Quincrux may have had a hand in my sentencing, but I can't be sure.

We came down from the roof together, me and Jack. Quincrux's smile faded quickly when we were greeted by a mass of reporters and a squadron of SWAT. It became obvious, very obvious, that he was only going to keep hold of one of us.

You can guess who he chose by process of elimination.

■■■

"Mail call!" Red Wolf bellows into Commons. He's not wearing the Native American getup today, thank god. "Bevins! Reasoner! Van Giles!" He whips the letters and cards at the boys. "Whitmore! Washington! Smith!"

He stops, rubs his pate, and then holds out two envelopes to me. I can't help but hope one of them is from Coco. It never is, but I can't stop myself from hoping. She's forgotten me, most likely. I can't blame her. But still, it hurts some.

"Cannon!" He smiles. "I see that you made some friends beyond these walls."

"Looks like, doesn't it?"

"Only you can let them keep you incarcerado." Red Wolf leans in and taps his temple with one long index finger. "In here, you are free," he whispers like a conspirator. He taps his chest. "And in here."

I look at the envelopes.

The first one, I tear open with eager fingers.

Shreveport,

I thought I'd send you a little something for your birthday. But I didn't know when it was. So I thought I might just send you something. Unfortunately, you're going to have to spend it all in one place.

Your friend,

Jerry A.

P.S. When you're out, come visit. I will buy your ticket. The missus doesn't like Double Shutter. And why should she? She always wins.

The card's stuffed with a ten-dollar bill. That's a couple Saturdays at the commissary, at least.

That Jerry. What a guy.

The next letter is larger, thicker. I open it, and a newspaper clipping falls out. Scrambling, I grab it off the floor before anyone can step on it.

Alleged "Twin Killer" Dubrovnik Dies in Jail Incident

Charles Dubrovnik, awaiting trial for over thirty charges related to the kidnap, rape, and murder of three girls, died in the Wake County Correctional Facility in an altercation between guards and inmates. Dubrovnik was found unconscious and rushed to UNC hospital. He was pronounced dead shortly after arrival. Police are withholding evidence until details of the incident can be determined.

On the back of the article, in red marker, is a *Q*.

I hate it that something Quincrux has done could please me so much. That I have murder in my heart. But there it is.

Not everything my mother said about me is true. And not everything Quincrux said was false. I've inhabited the minds of so many people—and had my own mind invaded so often—that the walls between black and white have crumbled. I don't really know where to stand anymore. I am them and they are me. The good folks of the world. And the bad.

I have to keep my bearings. I have to remember the darkness.

But the world is a little safer today. I hope Elissa has regained her place among the living. That she's warm and surrounded by light and laughter. That the part of her that can love hasn't been burned away or left in that pit.

I unfold the letter. It's written in a clumsy script. All the extra fingers must be hell on penmanship.

Shreve,

I don't have much time to spare for writing—they keep us pretty busy here—but I wanted you to know that I am well and have found a place where I belong.

After what happened on the roof and we were separated, Quincrux got us to his car using what they call a glamour. Not like the fashion term. Like a spell or something, I guess. I don't really understand all the psi stuff. I'm purely telekinesis-track. Which is the equivalent of being a jock in high school, at least here. Can you imagine that? Me, a jock?

I'm sorry I can't tell you where I am. I want to . . . but I can't. I mean, I physically can't do it. I can't make my hand write the word on this paper. I know it, I can spell it out loud, and I can say it. But every time I try to write it, I'll find myself staring out the window or biting my fingernails or tying my shoes and there'll be nothing on the paper.

There are other kids here. And older folks, like 25 or 30. Quincrux runs everything, and he's still the same. Really polite and scary. His politeness seems rude, somehow. But he makes a big deal about being nice to me. That doesn't make anything better, I know. He tried to kill you . . .

There's nothing I can do. He tells me he's going to leave you alone, but I can't make myself believe him.

I don't know. My brain is always foggy around here. I can't remember things. Things I know I should remember.

But I'll never forget you.

Please consider coming to us. Quincrux says he can have you moved here, but you have to want to come. Because of your "notoriety"— his word—you've attracted the attention of undesirables.

Be careful, Shreve. The witch isn't here. I know something happened to her, but I can't remember exactly what.

Anyway, here's a picture of me—yeah, I know, I've put on some weight, but some of it is muscle! I'm a jock, remember? Ha!— and there's a number on the back you can call at any time, and someone will come and get you out of there.

Think about it.

Your friend,

Jack

The picture is a Polaroid, thick and yellowed at the edges. Jack and a girl stand in front of a small tree ringed by industrial—military, even—buildings. Jack and the girl are holding hands. He's filled out some, and his hair is long and hanging into his eyes. He looks washed-out and a little worn. I can't tell if that's because of the photo quality or something else.

The girl stares into the camera. She's a pretty brunette, slim and willowy, unsmiling, one hand raised as if in greeting or in a gesture to the camera operator.

She has six fingers on her hand.

■■■

At the end of the day Booth escorts me back to my cell, frowning. He wants to say something, but it doesn't look like he's going to be able to spit it out before we get there.

"What do you remember?"

"Huh? Whatdya mean?"

I sigh. "You've been brooding since I got back here."

He stays silent.

"Listen, Booth. I don't know what he did to you. But it was real. It happened. And if you can . . . I don't know . . . sense things now, if you can pick up—"

"Pick up what?"

I stare at him. He's not manicured anymore. He doesn't glisten with pomade. His mustache isn't perfectly trimmed. His chest has lost its arrogant puffiness.

"Just try to remember. And when you have questions, I'm ready to answer them."

We stand like that, looking at each other, for a long time. Then I can tell that something in him relents, and he nods almost imperceptibly.

I turn and enter my cell.

■■■

It was a good day, Saturday.

When she came into the visiting area, her eyes were red, as bloodshot as a vampire's, and it didn't take a mind reader to know she'd been drunk not long ago. But she was dressed as neatly as I can recall seeing her.

Vig was holding her hand, smiling and hopping up and down.

I hugged them both, and my heart grew and for a moment I felt like I was moving out into the wide blue yonder, knocked out of my body by pure joy. I thought I was going to blubber like a titty-baby, but Vig grabbed my shirt and tugged.

"Lemme see the scar, Shree! Lemme see! Did it hurt when she stabbed you?"

And I never believed it would be possible, but at the thought the Dubrovnik woman had done something that might bring me closer to my family, I could hardly contain myself. I laughed.

▪▪▪

We're born into pain. We live in it, our constant companion through life. And when, finally, we shuck off this prison, we're free of it. For a while, at least, until we're reborn into the world.

But there are times of joy. Times of lightness and happiness. For now, I'm content being incarcerado. I'm content with Casimir, and Booth, and my cell.

Going to the mattress, I lift it up, dig underneath. When I first returned, I thought they tossed the cell, but all my stuff was here, exactly in its place. I've got a sneaky suspicion it's courtesy of Assistant Warden Horace Booth. I remember when he said, so long ago, "*That means I'm your daddy*," and pointed at the *Parens patriae* engraving above the Commons entrance.

It takes a moment, but eventually my hand finds the glossy surface and I withdraw the comic. Run my simple, five-fingered hand over the cover, the beautiful floating woman on the cover, shooting arc lighting from her eyes.

I climb up onto the familiar springs of my prison mattress, and I try to imagine Jack sleeping in the bunk below, his breath rising and falling in time with mine.

The air-conditioning kicks on. The vent near my head hisses and gives a hollow hush, and the black blows out, covering me like a shroud.

I sleep.

And dream of Maryland.

ACKNOWLEDGMENTS

As always, I want to thank my wife for supporting me through the good days and the bad. I would also like to thank my children for being so happy for me and interested in Shreve, Jack, and Mr. Quincrux, who have all assumed monumental proportions in their minds. Most likely because I won't let them read this book until they are old enough not to emulate Shreve's attitude. I fear I'm already too late on that score.

Of course many thanks go to my agent, Stacia Decker, for having such a fine sense of the saleable. And fashion. But the saleable pays the bills. The fashionable is just easy on the eyes.

When we were shopping this book around, Stacia informed me that Andrew Karre, head of Carolrhoda Lab and this book's editor, wanted to have a telephone conversation with me regarding *The Twelve-Fingered Boy*. After chatting with Andrew, I hung up the telephone with huge a sense of excitement for the possibilities of this book. And I knew this was the best home for it. I'm truly blessed to get to work with so many incredible people in my career and very glad that Andrew was there to help me take Shreve and Jack to where they needed to go. This book wouldn't have been the same without him and the rest of the great team of folks at Carolrhoda Lab and Lerner Publishing Group.

I'd like to thank all my buddies who did so many wonderfully stupid things at Pulaski Heights Junior High, especially Craig Hodges and Stephen Reasoner.

I'd like to thank all of those pre-readers who gave me encouragement upon reading this, my first young adult novel, especially Erik Smetana and C. Michael Cook, who've both been staunch supporters ever since we were stomping the boards at Zoetrope together. I also want to thank Kate Horsley and Julie Summerell for being wonderful ladies and fantastic pre-readers.

The Casimir Pulaski Juvenile Detention Center in this book (and all its staff and wards) is purely a figment of my imagination. When researching this novel, I realized very early that I wanted my juvie to resemble something more like a penitentiary than anything else, and, so, verisimilitude and the story soon parted company. Don't take this at a literal representation of how the juvenile rehabilitation system works here in Arkansas. In many ways it's better, though in some ways, it's worse.

And thanks, Mom and Dad, for always being there for me.

ABOUT THE AUTHOR

John Hornor Jacobs is the author of two adult novels: *Southern Gods*, which was short-listed for the Bram Stoker Award for First Novel, and *This Dark Earth*, which award-winning author Brian Keene called "quite simply, the best zombie novel I've read in years." Jacobs lives with his family in Arkansas. Visit him at www.johnhornorjacobs.com.